USA TODAY BESTSELLING AUTHOR

SARAH BRIANNE

SALVATORE

MADE MEN

Young Ink Press Publication
YoungInkPress.com

Edited by CD Editing
and Diamond in the Rough Editing
Cover Art by Young Ink Press

Connect with Sarah,
facebook.com/AuthorSarahBrianne
instagram.com/authorsarahbrianne
youtube.com/sarahbrianne-author
tiktok.com/@authorsarahbrianne
SarahBrianne.com

I dedicate this book to the Dolan County Texan Officer who wrote me a ticket for going 11 over the speed limit on the way to the Motorcycles, Mobsters & Mayhem book signing. So you know, my cruise control was set to 10 over, not 11.

Anyway, I'm hoping writing this means I get to write the speeding ticket off on my taxes.

And if you're wondering ... Yes, I am a petty bitch.

F rom the day Sal was born, his mother had told him she knew he had been born special. It had been a full moon the night he'd come into this world, and it only bore significance because there was an old family superstition that every Lastra had been born under one.

It wasn't until he was around four years old that she mentioned the second part of that story ... that every Lastra had also *left* this world under a full moon.

Why was it that she considered him to be the most special Lastra of all? Because it wasn't just a full moon he'd been born under.

It'd been a blue moon.

Rare. Unique. Exceptional.

All the things said to those born under one, and his mother swore the old wives' tale to be true. And since he was an extra special Lastra, who had been born under a blue moon in a special place of Kansas City that was named Blue Park, she said his fate of leaving the Earth would be under one, too.

This was a spectacular story to hear as a boy, and even

though he wanted to continue believing the grandness of it, he couldn't because, well ... his mother did drugs.

Yeah, so, *special* might not be the correct word to describe Blue Park, but maybe more so— hell. But even though his life was shit, as he spent his existence on and off the streets with her, depending on her addiction, he never begrudged her for the habit. He understood why she did it as the only way she could cope after working the corner for hours on end to wake up in a dirty motel bed with a different man every morning. It was to forget. Or to numb. That, at nine years old, he wasn't yet sure of, as his mother kept him far from the streets after dark.

Every day before a moon could come out, she gave him a couple of bucks just so he could safely stay at a twenty-four-hour Internet café. He never had the heart to tell her that it didn't even buy him an hour of use, so he always pocketed the cash and saved it until he could buy them something special to eat that wasn't from the garbage, or a can, or a bag of fast food.

The owner of the café, Terry, had become a close friend to him. Knowing exactly who his mother was, as Isabella Lastra was known as the town whore, he always offered him a warm place to stay the night in the back.

Terry was who he had gotten his love of computers from, and in return for his kindness, Sal never slept much, helping to clean the café at first then finally learning how to keep every device in there running in tiptop shape.

Any free time with Terry, they spent playing video games or doing his favorite thing ... searching the secrets of the world wide web. That was only allowed under special circumstances, like when a customer would come in and break the equipment.

Terry would find out where they worked, lived, and

even if they had also done another bad thing, then show up and make them pay for the damages. That went on for a while until two men showed up at the café late one night.

One guy who usually stood toward the back and never spoke always wore a brown leather jacket with fur around the collar. His name was Anthony, and the only reason Sal knew that was from the one time the older one of the two told him it was time to leave.

That one was Lucifer Luciano. Sal never had to be told who he was. Everyone on this side of the tracks knew about him. He was the scariest *motherfucker* in town, or so everyone always said.

If his mother ever knew Lucifer frequented the café, she would have never let Sal step foot in there again, as she had always warned him to stay far, far away from that man, because he ate little children.

He didn't. Or, at least, Sal didn't think he did. The first time he saw Lucifer, he got scared to death he might actually eat him, and it wasn't the crack his mother took after all that made her say those crazy things until Lucifer shooed him away with the wave of his hand.

It wasn't until they had left that Terry told Sal that whenever they came in the door, he was to go in the back and stay out of sight. So, every time he saw Anthony's coat come in the door first, Sal ran to the back like he'd been told before Lucifer could see him again.

He never could help but remember before Lucifer had whisked him away the first time they'd met how deeply he had looked into Sal's eyes. The black, devilish eyes Lucifer held had bored into his as he asked for his name.

With Sal too frightened he was about to be eaten to answer, Terry had told him, "Salvatore Lastra."

From that moment on, it was like Lucifer couldn't look

at him, nor stand the sight of him. Sal got off easy, he supposed, 'cause every now and then, he was able to listen in when their voices rose on the other side of the door. Terry would most likely have a black eye when he finally could come out after they left, and he always felt bad upon seeing it. Like it was somehow his fault, even though he knew it not to be true. It was only when Lucifer asked him to use the web for something Terry didn't believe was right.

It wasn't until one day when Terry was distracted that Sal entered Lucifer Luciano's name on the Internet like he had seen Terry do a bunch of times and found out just how dangerous Lucifer was. He didn't know what some of the big words meant that he had been accused of, like *racketeering*, but one Ask Jeeves search let him find out it was a common thing among criminal organizations.

Being sent down a rabbit hole, he found out the Lucianos were an alleged mafia crime family, which then led him to finding out Kansas City was lucky enough to have not *one* but *two* crime families.

The Lucianos and the Carusos.

It was another fateful night on a full moon when Sal finally got to meet a Caruso ...

"You sure you don't want some pizza?"

Sal shook his head back and forth at his friend, trying not to inhale the glorious scent while his stomach growled loudly.

"Your mom's not here, kid." Terry held the slice out to him, wanting him so desperately to take it. "She's not going to know you ate something without her."

As hard as it was, Sal held strong. It was impossible for him to enjoy a good meal without his mother. He always felt too guilty after, knowing his mom was most likely starving out in the cold right about now.

"No, thanks."

If he was lucky, Terry wouldn't finish the pizza, saving at least two slices. Then, and only then, would Sal take the cold pizza when morning came, for him and his mother to enjoy together.

"Suit yourself," Terry said, taking a bite of the pizza he held out before the little bell over the door could be heard.

A man walked in who Sal didn't recognize, and for some reason, he knew he wasn't a customer. Probably because the suit he wore was too fancy for Blue Park. There was no way he belonged here and must've been from the other side of the tracks.

"Sal, get to the back," Terry whispered to him, but it was too late, as the rich-looking man had caught sight of him already.

It was the same look Lucifer had given him when he'd first seen Sal. The look in their eyes as they met his told him they knew a secret that wasn't held on the web. What that was, Sal couldn't figure out. For now, at least.

The man's ice-blue cold gaze held him in place. "Who's the kid?"

You could tell Terry thought about lying, but despite his mother's job, Sal was proud of his name.

"Salvatore Lastra," Sal answered rather proudly, puffing out his chest.

"Nice to meet ya, kid." A big sneer appeared on the suited man's lips, making Sal think maybe it was him who ate children, before a firm, tanned hand came out in invitation to shake toward his face from the man. "Dante Caruso."

WHAT'S HIS NAME?

Valerie waved to one of her neighbors who lived across the street. The single mother was friendly and helpfully reminded her when she forgot to put the trash out.

Unlike him, she thought, driving past the neighbor who lived right next door as he removed his mail from the mailbox in front of his house.

Parking in her driveway, she grabbed two grocery bags then closed the car door with her foot before walking to her house.

An irritating imp that lived inside of her came out to play when she saw her neighbor walking back to his house without even bothering to say hi to Katie, who was the other neighbor, or her; it set her imp off.

"'Sup, Sal!" she yelled obnoxiously. "How ya been?"

The only reason she knew his name was because Katie had told her when a package had accidentally been delivered to her house.

Sal came to an abrupt stop at her yell. "Fine."

Fine? What kind of an answer was that?

She wondered how he could walk with that big fucking stick up his ass.

"I'm good, in case you wanted to know." Giving him a butter-wouldn't-melt-in-her-mouth grin, she jiggled her bags until she was able to put the key in the lock of her door.

Sal looked at her over the top of his glasses, as if trying to remember who she was. She was tempted to remind him that she had lived next to him for the last six months.

"Glad to hear it."

Did the dude ever smile?

Curtailing her imp from continuing to pester the man, she went inside her house and shut the door behind her with a shove of her shoulder. He could have at least kindly asked if she needed any help.

Placing the heavy bags on the counter, she started putting the groceries away.

She grabbed two handfuls of MoonPies and shoved them into her snack drawer, leaving it open. To save time, she decided to just tilt the rest of the bag's contents into the drawer before shoving it closed with a *thud* from her hip.

Quickly, she put away her almond milk in the fridge before opening the freezer and stacking all the frozen dinner meals she had purchased neatly inside.

She closed the freezer, folded up her reusable bags, and put them away. Then she finally took a blue Powerade out of fridge before she went back to her snack drawer to stare down at her assorted treats.

"Decisions, decisions ..."

Choosing a banana-flavored MoonPie, she carried both into her room to make herself comfy at her computer. She put on her bulky pink headset and returned to the game she had been playing before going on her grocery run.

"You there, Valkyrie?" a guy immediately asked.

"I'm here," she answered Justice on the mic.

"You get your MoonPies?" he joked as he skillfully gunned her down in the game.

"You know it. If you had bought the house next to me when I told you to, I could have tossed you one out the window."

Male laughter sounded through of the headset.

"He must be there. You only say that when he's there for the weekend."

"Just saw him," she confirmed, taking out one of his men in a blaze of glory.

"Has his date showed yet?"

"Nope. Usually, his entertainment for the night doesn't show until closer to seven."

"You got his timetable down pat. You stalking him? That's a punishable offense, you know."

"Don't have to." She shifted her eyes from her game to look out the window toward the house next door. "I can kinda see his front door from where my computer is."

The room she sat in was at the front of her house, while the window she sat in front of faced the side his house. Her house also had a bit of a smaller front lawn, which allowed her to view more of the front of his house, including his driveway. From what she could tell, his home had a strange configuration, where the front door indented into the home, giving her a sideview of his front door. From a window on the side of his house, she had tried her best to see through the blinds, and her best guess was it was his living room.

"You could try putting the computer facing *away* from that direction."

"I wish. My house is old as hell. This is the only outlet that won't trip the breaker from my setup."

"You could also put your setup in another room ..." Justice suggested.

Valerie rolled her eyes. "Geez, I should have thought about that."

Taking out two more of his men, she successfully took a dive off a building to land on another high rise. "All of the outlets in this house are fire hazards. When I sell this game, I plan to rewire this shithole."

"Have you heard back from Game Hookup?"

"Not yet." Pressing a button on her controller, she blew a bubble. Once it was large enough, she stepped inside to float down to the ground. "You think that's a good sign or a bad sign?" she asked.

"Dunno. I guess you'll have to wait and see."

"I wait much longer, I'm not going to be able to buy my MoonPies. I've already had to switch from Little Debbies to Great Value."

"I bet that hurt."

Grimacing as Justice destroyed half her team, she ran into the closest building to restock her weapons. "I still have my team."

"I meant giving up your Little Debbies."

"Oh ... it's not too bad, but the Nutty Buddies definitely don't taste the same. But I refuse to give up my MoonPies."

Looking over the edge of her computer, she saw a tiny sports car pull into her neighbor's driveway. "My neighbor's date is here, right on time."

"Damn, Valk, you were right on the nose." He cleared his throat before continuing curiously. "What does she look like?"

She took a vicious bite from her MoonPie, some crumbs spewing out with each descriptive word. "Blonde, big boobs, and looks like she came out of a centerfold. Dude is more predictable than the news. He only stays in his house for one weekend every other week, gets laid, and then disappears into thin air for another week."

As she talked and chewed, she was methodically taking out his team until Justice was the last one remaining and his avatar disappeared into a building before she could take him out.

"Why don't you like him? He sounds like a perfect neighbor to me."

"Dude has to be a cheater. Why else would he rent a house to stay only for one weekend every other week? He doesn't get any mail other than ads. Or a package that gets delivered when he's staying there."

"His behavior does seem shady."

She knew, for Justice to agree, that meant something.

Using her controller, she moved her avatar, searching for him. Was he waiting for her to come into the building to take her out?

She stealthily made it to the building Justice had gone into and was about to equip her X-ray vision goggles when Justice jumped down on her.

"Nice move," she complimented the other gamer.

His laughter sounded in her ear. "Nah, you're just paying more attention to your neighbor than the game."

"Not true. I couldn't care less what he's doing." Despite her words, she couldn't help herself from shifting her eyes back to the window to look at his house. "I wouldn't even know his name if Katie hadn't told me."

"What's his name?" he asked.

"Salvatore. Salvatore Lastra."

INTO THE BACK OF THE COP CAR

"Like I said, more predictable than the news," she huffed when the glow in the blinds went out. "Lights out?" Justice laughed.

"Mmhmm." It was between Sal, the bimbo, and God what they were up to now.

"Speaking of the news ..." Her online friend broke into her lewd thoughts, bringing her back to the game at hand. "Have you seen the news today?"

Skillfully, she sniped an opponent down on the other side of the map. "No. Why?"

"There was a cyberattack at the Horseshoe."

"That's not surprising," she grumbled before she took on a bit of a karmic laughter in her tone as she continued, "I told them for months we needed a serious upgrade in our firewalls."

The Horseshoe was a casino in downtown Kansas City that Valerie had been employed by for almost a year before she got the boot for opening her mouth too much about the lack of cyber security. She was young and newly graduated from college with her IT degree when she'd started working there, and unfortunately for her, being young wasn't the only thing that caused the senior members not to listen to her ... She was also a girl. Even in video games, she was in enemy territory. Numerous amounts of times she had been told, "Be careful not to break a nail," or worse, "Get back in the kitchen."

Males lacked serious creativity with their humor, and it wasn't until she was matched in an online game with Justice that she actually gave out a chuckle when he cussed her out about not picking up the health stick to revive him in a game. He had at least treated her like any other player, not like a girl.

Valerie was sure, like in most male-dominated fields, women were severely misjudged and not listened to. She had been obsessed with computers by the age of four and could build a PC by the age seven, but no one at her place of previous employment even cared to learn what she was capable of. Hell, she could have fixed the cybersecurity in an afternoon after coming back from lunch if they had let her, for no extra pay to her salary. Instead, the Horseshoe would most likely go bankrupt before they could afford another company to fix the fuckup now.

It was never good to fix it *after* the attack, with all the work you needed to do to repair the firewalls and start over with all new logins, passwords, and security, not to mention the lack of trust you'd lose from your customers.

Their competition across the street, the Casino Hotel, would chew them up and spit them out. It had stood there since the dawn of the city, and only the newness of the newly remodeled Horseshoe brought people in to gamble for the last year. The new owner was an I-D-I-O-T who used all the renovation money to make it look pleasing to the eye while totally ignoring the important infrastructure ... like upgrading the cybersecurity.

She didn't know why they even bothered hiring her in the first place. The dinosaurs still employed by the casino matched the infrastructure. Her boss, the head of IT, Edmond, finally kicked her ass out before she had worked there a full year when she showed him a simulation of what she could do to fix their firewalls. Now Valerie was shit out of luck for getting a good reference, and it didn't look good on her resume that her only place of employment in IT was for a job for less than a year after graduating.

Getting fired from your first big-girl job was just simply a bad look.

All she had to hope for now was for Game Hookup to literally hook her up by wanting to buy her game that she had been working on since she'd started college.

"Well, you were right. They've been shut down completely. Anyone who was gambling there since the attack this morning is still trying to get their money out of the machines."

"Good. I hope no one steps foot in the Horseshoe ever again," she said with no remorse as she showed the same respect to Justice when the head of his avatar landed in her crosshairs.

"Dammit," Justice huffed. "You got me."

Grabbing a Twizzlers from the now half-eaten bag, she placed the end of the red twisted candy in her mouth and tore it. "Up for another one?"

A yawn could be heard through the mic. "It's pretty late. I got work in the morni—"

"Oh, come on, Justice. We have to at least break the tie."

"Fine," he gave in. "One more. But I mean it; that's it."

Tearing off another bite of her stick, she began setting

up the next game and taking out some of the health and other helpful items on the map to make it harder. They had been playing all afternoon and into the night, but she was going to make this one count.

She was about to press *Start* on the game when she first heard it. When she looked out the window, the flashing blue and red lights off in the distance told her she wasn't imagining the sounds of the sirens.

"Is that police sirens?" Justice asked, now hearing them through her headset.

"Yep. What the—" Valerie stared out the other window in the room that faced the street. "Oh my God."

"What? What is it?" He knew he was about to get some juicy intel based on her reaction.

She had to blink at what she was seeing to make sure she wasn't imagining the scene. "They just parked between our houses. *Holy hell*, I think they might be going after Sal!"

"Are you serious? No way!"

Suddenly, Valerie swallowed hard at what she was witnessing now. "Um, Justice ..."

"Yeah?" You could practically hear Justice sitting excitedly on the edge of his seat.

"They're heading toward *my* front door—" Her voice came out a bit strangled with fear. "Not his."

Stunned silence met her on the headset, followed by the knock on the front door that had her jumping out of her gaming chair.

"Valk ... Valkyrie," he called out when she didn't respond as she took her headset off. Placing it on her desk, she could still hear his tone turning serious as he yelled over the mic, "Don't open your mouth! Don't say shit—"

As she walked to the front door, she tried to remind

herself, *Be cool. You didn't do anything wrong.* But why couldn't she help herself from feeling like she did?

Upon opening the door, she somehow made her voice as cool as her thoughts. "Can I help you?"

It was the biggest and scariest cop who spoke. "Valerie Monroe?"

"Yes?" she managed to strangle out, her coolness running out quickly.

The cop took her wrist in a tight grip, and before she knew it, cold metal was tightening on her skin. "You're under arrest for the cyberattack on the Horseshoe."

"I'm *what?*" With all collectiveness completely lost, the cop kept speaking, giving her her rights.

"You have the right to remain silent. Anything you say can and will be used against you in a court of law. You have the right to talk to a lawyer for—"

The haze Valerie went under no longer let her hear the words the cop spoke to her. Everything spun and became blurry in the flashing blue and red lights, and before she knew it, she was being shoved into the back of a cop car.

All alone in the back seat, she couldn't help but feel like a caged animal as she stared through the metal gates and right at Sal's front door.

The flicker of light had her shaking her head. The glow of the light in the window had returned.

Her stomach managed to sink even lower. She realized he had witnessed the most embarrassing moment of her life, along with Katie most likely, and all her other neighbors.

Even though Valerie didn't commit the crime she was being accused of, she no longer needed to worry about rewiring her house. She would be moving first fucking thing if she was lucky enough to get out of this mess.

She released a small sigh of relief when the driver's door

finally opened, hoping they could leave before the whole goddammed neighborhood woke up.

But, alas, her embarrassment had only just begun as the front door she was ominously staring at through the gates opened, and the only thing she could do was watch in horror as Salvatore walked right toward them.

MISTER FUCKING ROGERS

"'**S**up Sal?"

Inwardly, Sal groaned. Buying what he thought was a peaceful house, on a peaceful street, in a peaceful neighborhood was starting to become not such a good idea. He should have known his neighbors on Prairie Drive would eventually become nosy as hell. It was why he had bought this house in the first place. His vacancy on the top floor of the Casino Hotel was feeling a bit crowded over the last few years, and his privacy was becoming nonexistent.

Almost hitting your thirties would do that to you, he supposed.

He had thought going from an apartment to a house where no one knew him would be better, but the young woman next door was making it not so by becoming a pain in his ass.

Joining the Caruso family at thirteen years old, and then the family business by eighteen gave him no privacy. There simply wasn't any when all the members of the mafioso crime family lived on the top floor of the family business. Not to mention Sal barely got any time off over the last few years, holding one of the most important jobs by being head of security of the Casino Hotel. And it wasn't the only thing he was known for these days ...

"The Great Salvatore" was a title he was coming more and more known by online. At first, he was only known by every geek, freak, and nerd, but now his hacking abilities were even becoming legend by those who could barely remember their password to login to their email. He was so good, it made him untouchable. To be completely known by your hidden identity while also barely hiding your real identity was an art in itself. Simply, there was no one better who could catch him. Well, as of yet, and that was how he got away with it.

"How ya been?"

Fuck. Her grating voice made him stop in place.

He tried his best at a friendly neighborly tone with "fine," but it was obvious by her response that he wasn't exactly Mister fucking Rogers.

"I'm good, in case you wanted to know."

Her false placated smile wasn't missed. His neighbor liked him about as much as he liked her, which he would never understand.

Wasn't he the perfect neighbor? Sal was hardly around due to his job's demands, only able to stop by for a weekend every other week or so. His yard was kept neat, and he never bothered them. What was there not to like? Hell, he wished he had himself as a neighbor. So, what was her fucking issue?

Tilting his glasses down to look at her over the frames, he watched her struggle with the groceries that she was attempting to bring in with a hint of satisfaction. "Glad to hear it."

As he watched her struggle to make her way inside, the bags full of MoonPies and TV dinners didn't go unnoticed. In fact, there was a lot that didn't go unnoticed by him.

Sal figured she thought he had no clue who she was, but he knew Valerie Monroe. He knew every neighbor on this godforsaken street before he'd even moved in.

On paper, this neighborhood was a dream. He should've known it was a pipe one when he was stupidly ecstatic for his privacy when someone had mentioned it had gone to market. No one on this street had any family connections, let alone so much as a speeding ticket, but what he didn't account for was their nosiness when he had signed on the dotted line.

Going into his own house, he took a nice, deep calming breath, grateful to finally be away from watchful eyes, at least from the people who knew him. He figured he should be grateful for that, because there was no way Valerie knew he was a part of the Caruso mafia family. If she did, she wouldn't be so blatantly staring at his house all night over her computer screen.

Turning on the small lamp set on a table in front of the closed blinds, he removed his jacket, tie, and dress shirt to reveal his sleeveless white undershirt, making himself more comfortable before he went to make something to eat. To his distaste, his and Valerie's diets were much alike when he was in the neighborhood for the weekend. TV dinners were the only thing he bothered to stock, as they didn't go rotten while he was away from his home.

When he finished the Amy's frozen meal, he wished he had a MoonPie right about now. Smirking at the thought of passing the stage of asking for milk and going straight to asking for a MoonPie from his aggravating neighbor made him imagine the shock on her face. However, it quickly vanished from his mind when there was a knock on his door.

Not bothering to see who was on the other side through the peephole, he expertly opened it so prying eyes couldn't view him before he snapped the door shut.

"Hi, Sal," the woman crooned upon seeing him. "I was wondering if you were ever going to give me a call."

Suddenly, it was like having a cat in heat step into his house. "Sorry, Samantha, I've been busy."

"How come I haven't seen you in the Underground recently?" she asked, wrapping her arms around his neck so he could get an eyeful of her tits.

He decided on telling her the truth; it was no secret why he was no longer allowed to step foot in the illegal casino set above the legal one in the Casino Hotel. "Boss won't let me."

"Oh, that's right." She smiled seductively, going for the belt at his waist. "I hear you're a very bad boy who likes to count the cards."

Watching the hot cocktail waitress from the Underground seductively pull his long belt free until she backed up in front of the lamped window, Sal stalked in front of her until his lips hovered over hers. "How about we take this into the bedroom?"

"You don't have to tell me twice." She smiled before going in for a kiss.

But before her lips could touch his, he flipped the light switch off on the lamp, knowing the wandering eyes next door would go rampant throughout the night.

And he would let them ...

"Sal! Sal!"

The hit to his shoulder, along with his screeching name, had his eyes opening to the flashing red and blue lights. Quickly, he got to his feet to peek out the darkened bedroom window. He couldn't see much, as his bedroom was on the opposite side of the house to Valerie's, but he could see enough.

"I think you're about to be arrested!" she cried nervously through tears.

"What?" Sal looked back at her like she was crazy. "No, I'm not."

It would be a cold day in hell before any Caruso ever got locked up behind bars in Kansas City.

"Oh my God." Samantha stood up to hurriedly grab her things in the dark. "I'm getting arrested!"

"Jesus fucking Christ," he muttered under his breath. The poor woman wasn't bright. When they'd made it back to the bedroom last night, he had quickly remembered why he had put off calling her. "No, you're not. Just stay put," he ordered before she could run out the back door. That was the last thing he fucking needed for his neighbors to talk about, knowing everyone on the street was up, looking out their windows like he was.

Oh shitttt.

Still half-asleep, he rubbed the sleep out of his eyes, not knowing if he was dreaming or not when he watched the snooping Jane being arrested.

Before Sal knew it, he was in his dress pants, undershirt, and shoes and stumbled to the living room to turn on the lamp, then moved to his front door; he just couldn't help himself ...

He put on his glasses. It was time for him to play the nosy neighbor.

Payback's a bitch.

A BEAUTIFUL DAY IN THE NEIGHBORHOOD

S tepping outside into the cold night air, Sal couldn't help but to look up toward the night sky to the moon. It had become a habit since he'd been a young boy, and tonight was no different.

No full moon.

Finally, Sal looked down, instantaneously catching sight of the big officer who was on the Caruso payroll. Technically, they all were, but he knew Officer Daniels by name. If the Carusos ever needed to scare someone straight with a cop, Daniels was who they called.

"Officer Daniels." He nodded curtly, expecting him to notice him, but it wasn't until Sal removed his glasses that he did.

"Oh, hey, Sal. Didn't recognize you there." But it wasn't the only reason he was shocked to see him. "You live around here now?"

"Mmhmm," he said nonchalantly, slipping the spectacles back on. "So, what's going on?"

Officer Daniels rested his hands on his belt. "Turns out

your neighbor might be the reason for all the commotion at the Horseshoe."

"Is that so?" He tried his best to peer through the cop car, but the flashing lights weren't letting him see the glorious sight of her sitting in the back. The front doors, however, were open, as the cops had just been about to get in before he approached. So, he did know one thing ...

She could hear, and knowing her snoopy ass, she was listening.

"That's so."

"Welp, glad to know you caught her." Yawning without a fuck to give in the world, he was ready to go back to his home for a peaceful weekend without Valerie watching his every move. "Good night!"

"Say, Sal," the officer stopped him before he could walk off. "You haven't noticed anything suspicious, have ya?"

His eyes went back to the doors of the car still ajar. *Should I? No ... I shouldn't, right?*

Devious thoughts ate at him to do it, but his code told him not to ever rat. If there was anything the mafia hated, it was rats ... but this wasn't a criminal matter for him; it was a civil one. One where every time he came home, his peace was disturbed time and time again. Those beady little eyes trying to catch a glimpse of anything set him on edge and, frankly, tonight had been the last straw.

Pushing his glasses up higher, he let his friendly neighborhood alter ego do the talking. "You know ..." Sal cleared his throat and raised his voice an octave higher so he was certain she could hear. "She was staring at her computer all night."

Officer Daniels smiled, pulling out a pen and notepad. "That so?"

"That's so." He nodded, watching him jot it down with

a clear conscience. How incriminating could it be to say that? Half of America sat in front of their computer for hours. So, being the good neighbor Samaritan, he figured he should drive it home a bit more ... "I mean *glued.*"

He had barely finished his sentence before a rage-filled scream of obscenities came from the car.

"That motherfucking, cock-sucking bitch of a mother-loving whore of a bastard!"

Officer Daniels' eyes grew wide as he watched his cop car begin to shake as she beat the cage with her feet before looking over at Sal.

Basking in the glory of his enemy's downfall for a moment longer, Sal raised his eyebrows appreciatively. "Feisty."

"Seems like it," Daniels said, moving to the car door. "And thanks, Sal. You have a good night."

"Oh, I will." He whistled the tune of *Mister Rogers* over her shrill screams and metal banging. "It's a beautiful day in the neighborhood."

LYING KEELED OVER IN THE BACK SEAT, EXHAUSTED from her rage, she began to inwardly curse herself for letting her imp get the best of her.

Well, she was a gamer after all. They tended to rage from time to time, and Valerie found herself no better than a man.

Before Sal had opened his big fucking mouth, she'd thought if she ever got out of this mess, she'd move, but *not* now. Nope. She skipped right over full-fledged embarrassment to straight-up fury. Now, if she did manage to escape this crucifixion, she'd make Sal regret the day he ever moved in next door to Valerie Monroe.

If he thought she annoyed him now, just wait until her ass got out of jail. She was going to be his worst fucking nightmare that would make the likes of Harlequin look like a joke to Batman.

Closing her eyes tightly, she made a promise to herself in a whisper, "I'm going to make him pay for that."

The ride wasn't much longer before the car pulled to a stop. The officers got out of the car before the back seat door opened; it was Officer Daniels who did the honors of pulling her out.

"Hey, Chad, why don't you go on in and find something to eat in the station. I can book her myself."

"You sure?" the other officer asked, clearly remembering her not-so-minor outburst.

"Oh yeah, I can handle this little one just fine," he said, giving her cuffs a good tug.

"All right, then." Chad nodded, wasting no time to go inside.

Valerie's heart sank as her skin went cold from being alone with the officer. She wanted to tell him she was all bark, no bite ... well, mostly.

Nervous, she shakily began pleading when she was pushed up against the cop car. "Listen, I don't plan to cause you any more trouble. I just let my anger get the best of me, is al—"

"It's not me you should be worried about," he gruffed out in a hushed tone.

"Huh ... What?" she asked, having not expected that. *Did he sound ... worried?*

"Do you know who you just fucking cussed out back there?"

She looked up at the officer dumbly, and if she didn't know better, she'd think she saw a bit of fear in his eyes.

Valerie practically laughed at the thought. "Who? My neighbor Sal?"

The officer looked around to make sure they were alone. "Salvatore Lastra isn't a name you should be laughing at, nor a man you want to fuck with, do you understand?"

Her humor quickly faded, seeing that it was fear held in the big man's eyes. But now the question was: Why was a man like Officer Daniels so frightened of a man like Sal?

Shaking her head, she just couldn't grasp it. "I don't underst—"

Taking her arm, he finally began leading her toward the precinct with his tone going even lower. "All you need to know is: pray you don't get out of here anytime soon."

"No." She looked back up at him, still in disbelief. "I don't understand why you're telling me this."

"Well ..." He began loosening his grip on her. "I figured if you're dumb enough to not know who Salvatore Lastra is, there's no way you're smart enough to do what they say you did."

Valerie's eyes widened as her throat went dry. She licked her lips, and her blood ran cold. "And if *I am*?"

"Then I'd say"—Officer Daniels gave her a sympathetic glance—"whoever framed you did a pretty damn good job."

THE NEW BOSS

Cracking his neck as he listened to Dante and Lucca instead of throwing himself from the high rise, he tried tuning out Lucca telling his father not to smoke in his office. Sal couldn't blame him; he was the head of the family since Dante had stepped down to his firstborn son. So, this office did technically belong to Lucca now, as he sat in the big chair behind the desk while his father sat on the opposing side for once.

And Dante's cigar smoke did in fact reek and would stink up the office long after Dante returned to his home.

"You know Nadia won't let me smoke in our house," Dante gruffed out, sucking the sweet cigar between his gruff lips like it was going to be his last.

A lot of changes had been made recently within the family. Dante had moved out of the Caruso family home to live with Nadia. And hell, they even had facial hair. Before, only Lucca was allowed to defy his father by having a beard, but not only did Sal let his grow in, Dante was fashioning his own. However, some things never changed.

Lucca pulled out a pack of cigarettes from his pockets and placed a stick in his mouth in a desperate attempt to mask the cigar smell.

Sal couldn't help but laugh.

Over the years he'd spent with the Caruso family, he had grown used to the smell of cigarettes, considering Lucca had picked up the bad habit at a young age. Being best friends, he really didn't have a choice but to get used to it. The cigars, though, he never could. They just smelled, well, old.

"Have you tried smoking outside?" Lucca asked ironically as he burned the end of the cigarette after flipping open his Zippo.

It was safe to say those words went down like a sinking ship ...

Thinking of something cheerful while father and son continued their arguing match, he thought back to last night. Was it bad of him to have enjoyed seeing Valerie getting arrested?

He sniggered internally.

Probably.

But who cares? He sure didn't.

His lips twitched at the memory of her cursing him out. He couldn't think of a better comeuppance than seeing the embarrassment on her face as she walked handcuffed toward the car. The joy he felt was so extreme he was thinking of going to confession when he got off work.

A frustrated Lucca put out the bud of his cigarette, ready to leave. "If you've just come to smoke, then I don't understand why I have to be in here."

That was the exact question Sal himself had all morning since his glorious weekend had been cut short when he was called early into work, and he was about to get his answer.

"I just wanted to talk about what happened over at the Horseshoe and make sure nothing like that could happen here at the Casino Hotel."

Dante's gaze had moved to Sal as he spoke, but it was Lucca who answered.

"Is that a joke?"

"No." His icy gaze went back to his son's. "Why?"

"For you to even question Sal's capabilities is offensive." His friend and boss continued speaking on his behalf. "You know exactly who he is."

While Sal appreciated the vouch of confidence, he did understand why Dante would ask, 'cause like his cigars, he was ... old. And the older generation just didn't understand computers.

"It's fine," Sal said, taking no offense. "I assure you that you have nothing to worry about. No one can crack through the Casino Hotel's firewalls unless it was me on the other side."

"Are we done here?" Lucca asked, clearly ready to wrap this up. But, as if on cue, a knock on the office door had them all turning their heads toward it.

"Come in," Dante bellowed, ignoring his son's cold glare as he continued making himself right back at home.

Kent Bryant walked through the door, spoiling Sal's good humor.

He had a healthy distrust in Kent. Lucca and Dante would use Kent's services when they needed legal expertise that other lawyers refused in fear of getting disbarred. Not to mention, Sal also had his own personal reasons for disliking him and was holding a grudge.

"Sorry, I hope I'm not interrupting."

"You're not interrupting. Come in, Kent. What are you doing here so early in the morning?" Dante's cold gaze slashed to Lucca's again as he tapped his ashes forcibly in an ashtray. "Someone suing us that Lucca hasn't yet told me about?"

Sal watched the battle between father and son brew all over again. To be fair, Dante's glare was more formidable. He had years of practicing it before Lucca had stepped into his shoes. That was where the OG generation prevailed over the new generation. They were some classy-looking, mean motherfuckers.

Lucca, however, was just a mean motherfucker.

"No, I spent the night here in the casino, enjoying myself at blackjack, and thought I would mix some pleasure with business before I get changed and go to work. I've lost my ass at your table, and if there were any legal advice you needed"—a cunning smile was pasted on the lawyer's lips— "I can write the loss off as a tax deduction."

"We're good," Lucca answered before Dante could.

Kent's disappointment was palpable, but he shrugged it off. "Oh, well, can't blame a guy for trying."

Kicking back in the chair, Dante crossed his ankles. "How much you lose?"

"Eh, couple grand or so."

"Have a cigar," Dante offered, reaching out to open his cigar box. "Sal, pour Kent a drink."

While Kent went to the cigar box to take out a cigar, Sal used the distraction to mouth the correct amount at Dante before going to the liquor cabinet. Sal's wariness of him always had him keeping a close eye on the lawyer's goings-on here. So, when his eyes landed on his security camera this morning to see Kent gambling at a table, he'd quickly gone through the footage before heading to Lucca's office.

Taking the open seat next to Dante, Kent sprawled his

legs out like the ex-boss' as he moved the cigar under his nose to appreciatively smell it. "Thanks."

Dante nodded agreeably. "The least I could do since you actually lost fifteen grand."

"You're keeping track?" Kent asked, biting the end of the cigar.

"Sal is." Dante nodded over to him. "Usually, you're in the black with us."

"Bad night." The lawyer shrugged, taking the lighter Dante offered while Sal set the drinks down on the table between the two men.

Resuming his position against the wall, Sal opened the window wider to let the putrid smell escape for both his and Lucca's sake. He would change his suit after he left the office and send it out to be dry cleaned.

Kent enjoyed his cigar for a few moments before speaking again. "A couple of the players at the table came over from the Horseshoe. They were saying the Horseshoe was cyber attacked?"

"They were," Dante confirmed happily.

It was no secret that, over the last year, the Horseshoe had been their biggest competition. They had recently remodeled, and while Dante liked the traditional feel of their historic Casino Hotel, some players enjoyed the next new thing.

The lawyer lifted his glass toward Sal in a mock salute. "I bet they're wishing they had *The Great Salvatore* protecting their assets."

Suddenly, Sal felt the three men's gazes turn toward him.

"The hacker was arrested last night, but arresting them won't undo the damage done to the Horseshoe and their credibility."

"Good to know." Kent gave him a satisfied smile, puffing on the cigar. "Whoever they were, you'd almost think they did you a favor."

Each man in the room looked back to the lawyer, conceding his point.

Picking up his glass, Kent drained the contents before putting out the cigar. Standing, he stared down at Dante. "I'd hire whoever took out my competition."

He laughed while he'd said it, pretending to mean it as a joke, but Sal could see the wheels already turning in Dante's and Lucca's heads.

"Well, I better get to work. I do miss being my own boss." The lawyer huffed out a sigh after raising his arm to look at his watch. "You all have a great day."

The three of them watched Kent breezily leave the office.

Dante gnawed on his cigar with clenched teeth. "Sal ..."

"Yes," he said, sensing what was coming.

"Get us everything we need to know about the hacker who was arrested last night."

It wasn't until the new boss nodded in agreement with the old one that Sal regretfully agreed himself. "All right."

"I want to know where he sleeps, eats, and shits," Dante continued.

"That's the thing ..." Sal had to clear his throat from keeping his spit from strangling himself. He seriously doubted Valerie was the hacker, but ... "It's not a he ... but a she."

Rarely was the old boss ever surprised, but Dante certainly was at that revelation.

His son, however, intently leaned forward, and Lucca's strange-colored eyes clearly showed his interest had been piqued. "Sal, why do I sense there's more?"

Because there was.

"And ..." The Great Salvatore wished there were a god to strike him down dead in this moment. "She's my next-door neighbor."

OBSTRUCTION OF JUSTICE OR SOMETHING

S al drove back to his house on Prairie Drive, determined to finish his glorious weekend while reminding himself along the way that it had nothing to do with Lucca telling him to hire Valerie. There was abso-fuckin-lutely no way Valerie Monroe was capable of the cyberattack on the Horseshoe. Hell, he had known it despite what he had told Officer Daniels.

The Great Salvatore knew a gamer when he saw one, and Valerie was exactly that.

From her colored hair that shined a brighter blue in the sun, the MoonPies she packed in every weekend, to her oversized colorful hoodies and the big clunky pink headset he watched her wear as she desperately peeked through the window.

Valerie was practically a walking billboard for the company Razer, and on her forehead was spelled "gamer."

So, when he pulled up to his house to find a police car had returned to hers, he was shocked to see what Officer Daniels was carrying.

Well, shit.

Huffing, he threw on his glasses, wondering if he was really about to do this, when he caught a closer glimpse of what exactly was in his hands. That was when he regretfully decided he was.

Sal got out of the car and approached the officer and got an up-close look to find his suspicions confirmed. The computer Officer Daniels held was a custom-built PC that even had him curious.

"Hey, Officer Daniels, how's it going?"

"Not too bad, Sal." He continued lugging the big thing toward his patrol car. "Just about to head to the station. Do you mind opening the trunk for me?"

Sal went for the trunk but found his fingers fiddling with the release button. "You know, I, uh ... could take a look at that for you and let you know what I find."

Quickly, Officer Daniels transferred the heavy thing to one arm, going for the trunk button himself to pop it open. "Oh, that's okay."

"I wouldn't mind," he assured him as he watched Daniels continue to set it in the trunk despite his best efforts for him to hand the fucking thing over.

"I'm sure you're busy—"

When Daniels went to swiftly close the lid, Sal stopped it before he could.

"*Really*, it would be no problem at all," he tried again more *persuasively* as Sal's eyes narrowed on the officer.

What in the hell is his deal? Usually, Daniels was their easy-going cop for things the family needed, but he seemed anything but pleasant today.

"Listen, if she really did what they say, then no one in your precinct is going to even be able to break into her computer, and she definitely wouldn't be stupid enough to leave a trail." Sal tried to level with him as he continued, "Well, not any that *they* could track."

"The sheriff will have my ass if I don't bring this in. He personally asked me to."

Officer Daniels had finished with a smile that Sal could see right through, considering his hand still stayed on the trunk.

"Oh, don't worry; Sheriff Calloway owes me a favor." Sal laughed, going to pick up the computer from the trunk. *"Big time."*

A hand placed on top the computer, Daniels kept him from taking it. "Let me just give him a call."

"Sure." Sal deviously smirked and let the computer go to place his hands in his slacks' pockets. "Please do."

Officer Daniels reached for the walkie on his shoulder. "Sheriff Calloway?"

They both waited for the sheriff to patch in with a staring contest until a rather hostile voice finally came through. "What is it, Daniels?"

Clearing his throat, Daniels asked his question while his eyes never left Sal's. "Sheriff, I got Salvatore Lastra here, asking to take a look at the girl's computer."

The sheriff's voice returned in a more mellow tone. "Let him have it."

Sal smiled confidently, rocking on his heels, having figured that would be the outcome on the account that he'd found out the sheriff was banging every woman under his jurisdiction with a badge. How none had caught on yet defied his imagination, but he assumed if one of his groupies finally did, he'd have a herd of women after him who carried a gun and knew how to use it.

When he went to pick up the computer this time, he wasn't thwarted by Officer Daniels as he placed it in his arms. There was nothing Daniels could do now, and he knew it.

They both did.

'Cause like the sheriff ... Sal knew Officer Daniels' dirty little secret, too.

"Have a lovely day, Harvey."

VALERIE PACED THE CELL'S FLOORS AS SHE NERVOUSLY bit each nail down to the quick. The ink still on her thumb pads had tasted rather bitter when she went for a hangnail and instead got a mouthful of leftover ink.

Never once in her life had she run into the law, and yet, here she was, a wanted woman for something she didn't even do but certainly could.

How was she going to prove she didn't do it when, to be fair, she would put her own name the highest on the suspect list?

She had motive ...

Recently fired.

And whoever did it had to be good enough to cover their tracks; not unless she herself got out would she be able to possibly trace who had done it.

Looking around her cell, she had to admit the chances of that weren't likely.

I'm fucked.

When she heard heavy footsteps coming from down the hall, she yelled out for what seemed like the millionth time. "Hey! Don't I get a phone call?" Coming close to the bars, she tried to get a look at the officer approaching as she continued her obnoxiousness. "Isn't it, like, obstruction of justice or something if you don't give me one?"

The officer came into view and stopped in front of her cell. It was the other one who had arrested her along with Daniels. Crossing his arms over his chest, he took in the sight of her. It was rather obvious by his facial expression that a day in prison hadn't done much for her appearance.

"I guess you could call it that."

"Yeah," she agreed boastfully, glad she'd paid attention to things other than video games from time to time. She pointed an angry finger at the officer through the bars. "I have rights, you know, and I'll also have you know I plan to sue every last one of you fuckers to kingdom come if you don't open this door and let me the hell outta here right n—"

"Your lawyer is here."

Shocked, Valerie eyed the policer officer distrustfully as the cell door clicked open. "How is a lawyer here for me when I haven't been given my phone call yet?"

"I don't know." The officer shrugged before snapping, "How about you ask someone who gives a fuck? You coming or not?"

Damn, this guy is definitely not *Officer Daniels.*

She tried to remember if she had heard of any abuse about the police department in the news but drew a blank. Concluding they knew she was as poor as a church mouse and must've given her a court-appointed attorney, she stepped through the doorway. She'd take any excuse to get the hell out of that cell, even if it ended in another line of questioning.

Each time they had brought her to be questioned, their pleasant demeanors had changed once she had only responded with "I want a lawyer, asshole."

Walking past other cells with inmates within, she wished she hadn't watched *Silence of the Lambs* so much. They weren't exactly friendly faces. A few, she wanted to know what they were in for so she could Google them when she got out. She wanted to make sure they lived nowhere near her vicinity.

They went through a steel door, and she was ushered down another hallway than the one she had been taken to before.

Officer Asshole swiped his ID in front of a screen, and when a loud *click* could be heard, the officer opened the door. Not knowing what to expect, she poked her head inside to see a man sitting at a table.

Before she could straighten herself up to walk through the door, she was shoved from behind.

"I don't have all day."

Tripping forward, she somehow managed to save herself from falling straight down on her face.

"Officer Dunbar, that was completely unnecessary."

The furious voice of the man who had jerked to his feet behind a table made the hair on her neck rise.

Officer Dunbar's callous expression turned smug. "Kent, you have twenty minutes." Snapping the door closed, he left her alone in the room with the other man.

"I'm afraid Officer Dunbar's behavior is my fault." Apologetically, he frowned, sitting back down on the chair. "He wanted you to be shackled before leaving your cell. I disagreed with him to his supervisor, and he took it out on you. Are you all right?"

"Yes." Geez Louise, if she knew public attorneys were this hot, she wouldn't have paid her parking tickets.

Blinking at his smile, she wished she had asked for a hairbrush before she'd left her cell. Most lawyers on television were old and tired-looking with gray hair. Even in in their younger years, no one would consider them sexy. This dude looked to be in his thirties, with bright blue eyes, and to call this one sexy would be an understatement. Staring at him without embarrassment, she memorized every detail about his face, picturing him as an avatar in another game she planned to design.

"Have a seat."

Shaking herself out of the sexy stupor, she slid the other chair out and took a seat. "Do you mind me asking who you are?"

Something about him almost seemed familiar, but when her breath hitched in her throat at his grin, she knew there was no way she had ever met him. There was no forgetting a man like him. And forget the parking tickets; this dude was worth committing a felony for. He was almost as good-looking as her neighbor ...

Remembering what he did last night, she took that assessment back. This dude was better-looking. He seemed like the type to at least help her in with her groceries. She was going to Google his fine ass, too. She could *definitely* see him as an avatar.

"I'm sorry. I was so angry at Dunbar I forgot to introduce myself. My name is Kent Bryant. I've been hired to be your attorney."

Reality rushed back at his introduction, and she grew confused. "So ... you're not a public attorney?"

"No, I've been retained as your attorney."

"By whom?" she asked, amazed. Valerie had zero money and no friends. *Well, at least in KC.*

"Lucca Caruso."

Her mouth dropped open. You couldn't live in Kansas City and not know who the hell Lucca Caruso was. The Caruso family owned the Horseshoe's biggest competition, right across the street, and recently, Lucca Caruso had become the CEO of the Casino Hotel.

"Lucca Caruso?" she repeated the name to make sure she had heard it correctly.

Mr. Bryant gave her an amused smile. "Yes, Mr. Caruso asked me to represent you."

"I'm not usually in the position to look a gift horse in the mouth, but are sure you've been shown into the right room?"

"Are you Valerie Monroe?" he asked, opening a plain file in front of him.

Stuttering, it took her a moment to get the word out. "Y-yes ..."

"Then I'm in the right room."

Past confusion, she wiped her sweaty palms on the thighs of her pants. "I didn't hack into the Horseshoe's computer system, if Mr. Caruso is afraid I'm going to attack his computers."

Was this room wired for sound? She lowered her voice to a whisper, her lips barely moving in case one of the officers was trying to lip read their meeting. "I wouldn't, even though I could," she added in a rush. "I would never, *ever* be stupid enough to try to hack into the Carusos' computers."

Kent's blue eyes dropped to her lips. "Why are you talking so weird?"

"In case they're reading my lips." Valerie used her chin to point to the camera on the wall.

Her lawyer looked at her as if she had stepped off a UFO. "Why would they want to read your lips?"

She wiggled her eyebrows at him, hoping he would get her meaning.

He didn't. He only looked more confused.

Valerie looked at him pityingly. *Did he not know who the Carusos were? And the poor hot thing worked for 'em, too. It would be a real shame if they ever tried to whack him.*

"The Carusos are dangerous." Making her voice barely audible, she told him while wiggling her eyebrows again, "Everyone in KC knows they have ties to the mob." Seeing him take the news differently than she'd expected, she suddenly narrowed her eyes on him. "Are you laughing at me?"

Mr. Bryant bent his head, seemingly to read the papers in front of him. "No."

"You sound like you are," she hissed. "Listen up. It's nice meeting you, but I'm going to decline your offer to represent me. I'll hire my own lawyer."

Raising his head back up for her to view, there was nothing on his expression that showed any amusement. "Do you have enough to pay a lawyer? There's going to be a hearing Monday morning to arraign you. The DA is going to ask for a two-million-dollar bail."

Her jaw dropped yet again. She wanted to cry at the fact she would be stuck here all weekend, but it seemed to pale in comparison to the fact of *two million dollars*!

"What the frick! I can't afford that!"

Mr. Bryant nodded. "I'm aware of the that fact."

"How?" Suspiciously, she stared at him.

"I researched you before I took your case."

Now, *this* was her kind of man.

"Your house was two hundred thousand when it was last listed, but you're behind on two mortgage payments, and your credit cards are in even worse shape. Currently, you have no source of employment. You're a flight risk with no known family in the area, or anywhere I could find. The Horseshoe is pressing charges, saying they lost over one point four million dollars before they could get their computers online. The DA wants to make an example out of you to keep others from attempting the same crime. He's going to go for the maximum sentence he can get."

With her throat slowly closing as each word passed his lips, she felt as if she couldn't breathe. "I'm going to rot in prison ..."

"Val—" He suddenly cleared his throat. "Ms. Monroe, are you all right?"

"Do I look all right?" Wildly, she looked around the room, feeling as if the walls were closing in around her. "I need to get out. I can't stay in here any longer! I need my Twizzlers!"

"Breathe!" Mr. Bryant started out of his chair then sat back down. "Dammit, put your head between your knees."

Turning sideways in the chair, she did so. It was a better option than passing out.

"Now take deep breaths," he instructed her firmly.

She did as she was told. The spinning sensation in her head eased, and she was able to catch her breath.

"Better?"

"Yes," she mumbled, her head still down. "Is a public defender going to be able to get me out of here?"

"No."

At the truth in his voice, her head started spinning again. "C-can you?"

"Yes."

Finally able to raise her head back up from her knees, she wanted to look him in the eyes to make sure he was honest with her next question. "Are the Carusos going to off me if you get me out?"

"No."

It was another simple answer from him and, while she believed him, her blood still ran cold. Owing Lucca Caruso a favor could never be good.

Yet, she had no choice.

"Then I guess you can be my attorney."

"Thank you. You made the right choice."

"I have *no* choice," Valerie corrected him. Straightening, she held on to the table for support as she began to lose it. "I need my Twizzlers. And my computer. I'll go nuts without them. I used to vape, but the Twizzlers kept me sane. Will they let me vape in my cell?"

She turned in her seat, looking toward the door. There had to be a way to bust out of this jail. She designed games; she should be able to figure out a way out of here. All the officers she had met so far were definitely not gamers, and she was Valkyrie ...

"No, they won't let you vape in your cell, but—"

Dragging her gaze from the steel door, she focused back on him, at his calm voice, to see him reach into his briefcase.

"I do have this. It was going to be my lunch. Do you like N—"

"Nutty Buddy!" Valerie practically snatched it from his hand. Ripping open the package, she could tell at first bite it wasn't the generic shit she had been eating recently, either. If she weren't too busy shoving it down her throat, she'd lean over and give him a big ole chocolatey, peanut buttery kiss.

"Listen, the police aren't going to let you near any computers, especially your own." He got back to business while she finished her snack. "And they've executed a search warrant. Are they going to find anything incriminating?"

She started fanning herself. "The only thing they'll find are the games I'm developing and the games I play." Nervously, she looked away while she continued chewing the last bite.

"That's all?" Kent Bryant searched her expression. The dude was giving her vibes he didn't believe her. He was slipping on his attractiveness scale. Why did he doubt her?

Her chest puffed out in indignation. "I worked for the Horseshoe before they fired me. They'll find some work-related correspondence," she admitted. "I warned them a kindergartener could get past their firewalls, and I was terminated for my trouble."

"That's all?"

His relentless stare had her sucking her chest back in.

"When I got fired, I *might have* sent the dude who fired me a tiny bug in an email ..."

Kent exasperatedly rubbed at his temples. "What *kind* of bug?"

"Nothing bad, per se ... Just ... every time my boss, Edmond, sent an email to other employees, the emails would also be sent to the CEO. I wanted him to find out that Edmond is undermining his authority. I tried to tell him that before I was terminated, but he didn't want to listen any more than when I had warned him about the firewalls. I sent another email the next day fixing the bug."

Her attorney stared at her stone-faced. He was much less attractive when he wasn't smiling. "You just made my job much harder."

To be fair, she had probably dropped in his estimation at her confession.

"It was just a harmless prank," she tried her best to excuse herself.

"The judge won't see it that way."

"The judge didn't have to work for the Horseshoe." She continued rather frankly, "They're dicks."

"Is there *anything else* you need to tell me?" he asked, clearly urging her to think hard.

"No ..." God, she needed her Twizzlers. "You got anything else to eat in the briefcase? Or a vape I can take a hit of?"

He shook his head before one of his eyebrows slowly rose. "You don't seem sure."

Damn.

Her shoulders slumped forward. She wasn't going to see any of those sweet red vines in her near future. "I think I need a break."

"Valerie—" he tried coaxing her again more forcibly, "is there *anything* else you need to tell me?"

She wanted to cry. The fantasy of him ever carrying her groceries in for her finally bit the dust.

"Not in the computer, *per se* ... But does taking their scrap computer parts count?"

THE AUDACITY OF THE MAN

Two million fucking dollars? She wasn't fucked ... Valerie was *royally* fucking fucked.

With it being Monday, she had officially been in jail for well over forty-eight hours, and the withdrawals were definitely starting to hit even more.

Hearing approaching footsteps, she thought she'd try again for the millionth time. "I'm starving! What's a girl gotta do to get some food around here?"

Officer Daniels came into view on the other side of her cage. He had been avoiding her all weekend, and she knew it, because he hadn't once looked in her direction when he walked down the hall, no matter how much she called out to him. However, his eyes traveling down to her empty food tray on the cell floor told her his time of ignoring her was over.

"You just ate," he said in exasperation.

"Okay, then ..." Those words had only set her off as she began correcting herself. "What's a girl gotta do to get some *good* freaking food around he—"

Her screaming came to a halt when Officer Daniels

unlocked the door, swung it open, and nonchalantly said through her tirade, "You're free to go."

Valerie rapidly blinked in shock and wondered if she'd heard him correctly. "What?"

He placed strong hands on his belt and took an intimidating step forward. "I said, you're free to go, Monroe, or would you like to stay here another night?"

"No, I—" She cleared her throat, trying to put her imp back in its cage and get her thoughts in order. "I don't think I do."

Heading to leave, she went to walk past the officer through the small opening but found his hand on her arm, stopping her.

Any intimidation tactics were gone. It wasn't Officer Daniels speaking but a concerned man. "You sure about that?"

She stared up at him in complete confusion. She would never, ever understand men. "You ignore me all weekend, and now you look like you want to help me when I'm no longer locked in a cage?"

"I-I—" It was clear he had no idea what to say, and him looking down at his watch followed by glancing down the hall where another cop could come through at any moment told her he had no time to say it if he did.

"Listen"—she appreciated the sentiment, but—"I damn sure don't think I want to spend the rest of my life here."

"There are worse things," he warned gravely.

Valerie swallowed hard at seeing the fear return to the big man's eyes.

"I thought I was free to go, though?"

"You are. For now, anyway," he explained. "But you might not be able to return even if they did convict you."

"I see," she whispered, taking a deep, calming breath, knowing exactly what he meant.

"I can say you tried to fight me; get you on assault of an officer if you're lucky."

"I'm not smart enough to let you do something like that, remember?" Valerie laughed, using his own words against him. Knowing there just might be some truth to them, she tried her best to put on a brave face as she pulled her arm out of his grasp. "Thanks for the heads-up."

As she walked away from the defeated officer, she felt the need to let him know one thing. "I really could have done it, you know."

He simply shook his head, still certain she hadn't. "You do this for as long as I have, you get pretty good at spotting them." When she didn't seem to follow, he continued, "Criminals."

She chuckled, offended. Almost. "I'll have you know I've stolen something before."

His eyes narrowed on her before they relaxed, clearly still not believing her. "Hope to see you around, Monroe."

"Yeah, me, too," she mumbled sadly, remembering his words. What he really meant to say was ...

You might not be able to return, alive.

She left the precinct to the warm sun shining down on her face and felt like a new woman. All she needed was a shower, a fresh set of sweats, her computer, and some Twizzlers, then all her problems would melt away.

Temporarily, of course.

She couldn't fathom how or why Lucca Caruso would pay her two-million-dollar bail, considering he didn't even know her and her lawyer had called her a flight risk, but she did know in her heart that he had, and that fucking terrified her. Again, that was a problem for another day. Today, she just needed to feel freedom once again.

On her way down the steps of the building, her smile slowly started to fade as she caught the old Coupe de Ville pulling up.

She knew the owner of the navy Cadillac before he exited the car, and if the windows weren't so tinted, she could have sworn he had put on his glasses before getting out.

To put it simply, Valerie stood in complete shock 'cause she could not believe *the audacity* of the man coming around to the other side of the car.

Lazily, he leaned against the car and folded his arms across his chest. "Hello, Valerie."

His nonchalant, fucking I'm-too-cool-for-you and I'm-so-much-better-than-you attitude sent her into a spiral when she was already teetering on a dangerous ledge.

"The hell are you doing here?" she screamed at him but didn't wait for him to answer. "Come to gloat? To see how I look after my weekend from hell?" She added in a higher screech, "Or have you come to give another statement? Well, here's one for you: go fuck yourself, Salvatore Lastra!"

Sal swallowed hard, squaring his jaw before it softened. "Okay, I might've deserved that."

"You think?" Her sardonic tone was followed by her simply walking away as she cursed him under her breath. "You motherfucking asshol—"

"Hey!" Sal had to quickly catch up. "Where are you going?"

"The bus stop," she answered him like he was an idiot before she continued her cursing. It was therapeutic. "You *dumbass* motherfucking asshole."

His voice had come out a bit strangled, and she didn't

miss his best try at attempting to sound like a friendly neighbor that was complete bullshit. "I thought I could take you home."

"I'd rather the bus run me over twenty-seven times before I'd ever take a ride from you."

"Goddamn." Even Sal was taken aback by that, standing frozen in place for a moment. Then he said, "Fine, then. I was just going to offer you a peace offering by buying you lunc—"

Valerie stopped in her tracks and spun on her heels. "From where?"

"Wherever you wanted."

She doubled back to his car, hitting his shoulder as she passed in a hurry to reach her destination. "You shoulda led with that."

A LARGE BAJA BLAST

There was no one in the world he hated more than Valerie Monroe right now.

"You want to go where?"

"Taco Bell." She pronounced the fast food place like he was a two-year-old and had just heard it for the first time.

"Of course, you fuckin' do," he mumbled as he regretfully pulled down the street where it was located. That and a bucket of chicken from KFC was any gamer's dream. "I thought you'd want to go eat inside somewhere? I'm buying, so you can pick anywhere you'd like. I mean *anywhere*." He emphasized the last word in a desperate attempt that she'd want to make him pay by racking up an expensive dinner bill. Money wasn't the issue. Hell, he had copious amounts of it, and he'd throw it at her if that was what she wanted. What he detested was the fast food chain that, frankly, he wouldn't serve to a dog.

Valerie gave him another look that questioned his brightness, and it was another thing he was starting to highly detest.

"I've spent a weekend in jail, Sal. Do you really think I look acceptable enough to eat at a nice restaurant?"

He gave her another once-over and debated on telling her he didn't think she looked much different than how he usually saw her. Sal decided against it, though, considering she was a fucking lunatic, but it appeared she had figured out his thoughts, anyway.

Her hand went to the door handle. "You know what? Just stop the car."

"I could take you back home to change first, if you'd like—"

"Stop the car!" she screamed at him.

I would love nothing more than to stop the fucking car! But he had to continue to play it cool. "I thought you wanted Taco Bell?"

"So, you're taking me?"

Christ, it was like dealing with a toddler. "Yes."

"Okay, good," she said, making herself too comfortable in the leather seats, enough to play with the buttons in his car. "I thought your car would look like a piece of shit on the inside."

"What? Why would you think that?" he asked, clearly offended. His car was a classic and meant more to him than a lot of things in life. It was the longest relationship he'd ever had. Hell, the only relationship he'd ever had.

She shrugged. "I don't know. I guess 'cause it's old."

"Just because something's old, doesn't mean it should be thrown out."

"Hey, I agree." Valerie held her hands up. "Just telling you what ninety-nine percent of the population would do, and they would have upgraded at least two times by now."

"Well, I'm not ninety-nine percent of people," he said,

leaning over to shut the glovebox before she could rifle through it.

Getting his message, she tried her best to sit still. "Oh, there it is, my beautiful neon lights."

He rolled his eyes heavenward as he pulled into the lot to park the car.

"Nuh-uh, we're going through the drive-thru," she told him, moving the wheel toward the long line of waiting cars. "I look like shit, remember?"

"Everyone in Taco Bell comes out looking like shit," he told her, trying to turn the wheel back.

"Is this my peace offering or not?"

A dark thought might have popped into his mind before his boss' face. That was when he decided to go through the drive-thru.

"Fine. But you're not eating this shit in the car."

Why it had seven cars lined up, he would never understand.

He rolled his window down as he approached the loud box, and Valerie leaned over him to order. He was able to get a better look of her up close. Her pale skin that desperately needed to see the sun carried some freckles that he thought were kind of cute, especially the ones on the bridge of her upturned nose. But when she talked, any and all cuteness about her was viscerally obliterated.

"Can I get two supreme Doritos locos tacos, an order of nacho fries, and a large Baja Blast? Oh"—she quickly remembered something else before she could finish her order—"and a Mexican pizza."

Dorito taco? Holy fuck, he was going to vomit. *Mexican pizza?* As an Italian, it was a fucking sin against everything holy.

When he pulled up to the window, a drink was already being held out to him.

"Here's your battery acid," he said, giving her the bright sea-foam green drink.

"How do you not like Baja Blast?"

He didn't even bother answering that he had taste buds. Instead, he handed the cash over to the guy in the window then took her food before driving off. He instantly regretted rolling up the window. This suit was going to be the next one off to the dry cleaners.

"What's your deal with Mexican food?" she asked, shoving her straw into the hole of the soda cup.

"I have nothing against Mexican food," he corrected her. "But Taco Bell isn't Mexican food." He wasn't even sure it was food.

It was clear she didn't totally disagree and stood corrected. "Okay, what's your deal with *Taco Bell*?"

"My deal with them is they put out 'new'"—he said the last word loosely and in air quotes—"food items every month, but they all literally taste the same; they just layer it differently."

She looked dumbfounded. "Holy shit, I think you're right."

Despite her mind being blown, she proceeded to open the bag and take out a taco. "So, you *have* eaten Taco Bell before."

"Many times," he said rather sadly, wanting to vomit at the memory that flooded his mind. The only good thing about it was the prices. At least back in the day.

Hearing the paper crinkling brought him back to the present. "What the hell do you think you're doing?"

Valerie opened her Dorito taco with no remorse. "Eating."

"You better n—" He couldn't even finish his sentence as he watched her take a huge bite, causing some of the lettuce and taco shell to spill everywhere. "You didn't."

"Oh, I did and am," she confirmed with another bite. "I was in that jail cell, eating slop and thinking about what you said *for days*. So, I'm going to enjoy this."

Sal gripped the steering wheel in a death grip. His suit wasn't going to be the only thing needing to be cleaned. He was going to be lucky if blood didn't need to be cleaned out of his car.

Out of all the ways she could pay him back for what he did, this was quite possibly Sal's worst fucking nightmare.

"You want a bite?" she asked, holding out the taco and sending more lettuce flying.

Sal's knuckles turned white. "I'm good, thanks."

"Suit yourself," Valerie said, moving on to the next taco.

By the time she had finished the second taco, her fries, and her pizza, Sal thought he was going to be sick. Not only was his car covered in crumbs, lettuce, and diced tomatoes, but so was he.

She sucked on the straw of her drink until it gurgled dry. "How'd you know I got out, anyway?"

"Officer Daniels told me."

"Oh, he did?"

He didn't. But she didn't need to know that.

Nodding, he wasn't sure she bought it but thought she must've when she continued her questioning.

"You going to tell me why you did it?"

He took his eyes off the road to look over at her. "Did what?"

"Make it seem like I was the hacker by giving Officer Daniels that statement." Her words came out annoyed.

"Do you really need to ask that?" Sal gave her an incredulous look, having to take his eyes off the road again, knowing she wasn't dumb in the slightest. Valerie was simply just annoying.

"I suppose not," she agreed, knowing she had gotten under his skin. "And do you think I am the hacker?"

Sal shook his head as he answered honestly, "No."

"Why not?"

If he didn't know any better, he'd think she was almost offended, but Sal knew before he had gotten a hold of her computer that she was innocent.

Smiling with satisfaction at the memory of her thrashing around the back of the cop car, he couldn't help himself. "Sweetheart, you'd have to be framed to have caused a scene like that."

G-O-O-D-N-I-G-H-T

Taking a ride from Salvatore Lastra was to her benefit. It made her able to eat food faster and brought her home quicker than waiting on a bus for an hour. It also gave her a chance to fuck with Sal for a bit and pay him back for what he had done to her.

Now that he had just pulled into her driveway, it was over, and she hoped to never have the pleasure of being in his presence again.

"Bye!"

Throwing herself out of his car, she went to her precious home, not even bothering to take her trash with her. However, that might've been her mistake as Sal chased after her.

"Hey, wait," he said, grabbing her bag of empty, smelly wrappings and drink from his car.

Valerie didn't bother looking back; she went to her front door but found it strangely locked. She lifted the well-used welcome mat she had bought from Goodwill. "You have a trash can at your place, I'm sure. Good day."

Not taking the hint, Sal watched her pull the key to her

front door from under her mat, appalled. "Christ, Valerie, you're a single woman living alone; why don't you just place the key *above* the welcome mat next time?"

"First of all, like you really care about my safety." She gave him a scolding look, wanting to shove the sharp metal object right up his ass. "That's real rich coming from you, considering you let me *rot* in prison over the weekend. And secondly, I have a boyfriend, thank you very much, and he's big. *Huge.*" She started sliding her key into the hole. She was almost home sweet home. "So, if you don't mind, I'd like you to leave me the fuck alone before I get my boyfriend to beat the shit out of you."

"Oh yeah, you have an online boyfriend? Where does he live exactly? Wisconsin?"

Her smile faded. They both knew she was full of shit. Turning the knob, she was ready to slam the door in his face. "Go fuck yoursel—what the fuck!"

Valerie and Sal stood at the front door with their mouths agape at the scene. Any trash in his hands was dropped to the ground in shock. Her whole house had practically been torn apart.

It took her a moment to get past the shock, and once she did, she ran right to her computer room with her heart beating out of her chest. She knew in her heart it was gone before she reached it. Still, nothing could have prepared her for it actually being gone. The only thing remaining was her computer desk that had been flipped over and lay broken.

Deadly silent with rage fueling her imp, she walked to the corner of her room and picked up the Harlequin cosplay bat that still stood leaning against the wall and gripped it tightly.

∞

THE SOUND OF A HARD CRASH MADE SAL RUN INSIDE her house and call out to her as he hurried toward the sound. "Are you ok—"

"Those motherfucking bastards!"

At the scene he stumbled in on, it was safe to say, *she's definitely not okay.*

Screaming at the top of her lungs, she beat at a flipped-over desk with a wooden bat that held bold red lettering. Sal wasn't one hundred percent sure, considering he could only catch flashes of the lettering, but he was pretty certain by the fifth swing it spelled out G-O-O-D-N-I-G-H-T.

"Those fucking cops took my computer, didn't they?" She stopped to ask, looking right at him as her knuckles turned white from her deathly grip.

In all his years devoted to the mafia, he had never been so scared in his life. "Yep. Mmhmm. Yes, they sure did."

"Those fuckers!" she screamed again, slamming her bat back down on the desk. "My whole life's work was on it!"

Sal stepped back a bit when a piece of flying wood bounced off his glasses. "Your life's work?"

"Yes, my video game." She hit down with the bat. "Bub-blegum Blitz." She slammed her bat down again. "I've been trying to sell it to Game Hookup the last few months."

"Oh ..." He lifted his fallen glasses up his nose, thinking back to him scouring her computer last night. Sal had not only opened the game, but he had played the fucking thing all night after getting sucked in. Since he hadn't played video games since before he joined the mafia, he no longer kept up with the newest games anymore because he never had the time. The game was so good that he had assumed it was one that not only had been released already but had been designed by a huge gaming company. "I see."

Thinking it was best to let her get it out of her system

and tire herself out, he let her get a few more hits in before he tried to step in. He held out his hands as he approached, and she stopped swinging enough for him to take the bat, and only when it was in his hands did he break it to her.

"Listen, they are not going to let you anywhere near your computer, as I'm sure it's locked away into evidence," he quickly added the last bit in a rush, too afraid to tell her that he was the one who actually had it.

"Yes, they told me I couldn't use any electronic devices and confiscated my phone, too," she admitted, clearly feeling dumb at her outburst. It was obvious she should have known her computer would have been gone.

"Okay, well, that would have been good to know," he muttered under his breath. "So, you just gotta work on proving your innocence ... without all that."

She patted her forehead; it looked like Valerie was about to faint. "I feel dizzy."

Sal quickly turned over her computer chair that had been left unscathed. The poor Ikea desk, however, was a total loss.

"Sit down. I'll get you some wat—" By the time he had finished setting the chair upright, she was tilting toward the ground. "Oh shit!"

Sal barely caught her in time before she hit the floor. Cradling her limp body in his arms, he found himself preferring her quiet and unconscious. He was able to study her up close again, seeing those many freckles that kissed her skin. She was awfully tiny for a girl who ate so much. Her small frame was soft in his arms, and he found himself wondering dangerously how she'd look without those heavy, thick, and oversized clothes.

She didn't dress to his taste, and as he tenderly brushed a rogue strand of hair out of her face, the fun color of it was another thing he didn't prefer on women. But, for Valerie, it suited her. Her dark blue hair shined like the ocean lit by moonlight. You could tell her look was inspired by her video games. It was just her, and Valerie was nothing but herself at all times.

"Valerie?" he cooed, stuck between wanting to wake her as he became concerned with how long she had been out and not wanting her conscious and speaking again. God only knew how the unpredictable and psychotic woman would react when she did wake in his arms.

Sal's worry only grew, and so he tried calling her name again. The slight, groggy moan that escaped her lips had him tightening his jaw. Not wanting to think he was possibly starting to become attracted to her, he patted her cheek, and his tone got harsher.

"Valerie?"

Lashes finally started to lift off her cheeks. "W-What happened?"

"You fainted."

"I w-what?"

She was clearly still a bit dizzy, so Sal thought it would be best to move her to a place she could better relax. Lifting her off the ground in his arms, he left the room in search of finding a safe place. He spotted the futon in the living room and went to lay her down gently on the rickety furniture. He really hoped this wasn't where she was forced to sleep every night.

Taking advantage of the closeness, she felt up his biceps, trying to squeeze hard through his suit. "Wow, you're stronger than you look."

Instantly, Sal reached for her forehead, thinking he might need to take her to the hospital. Valerie had to be critically ill to give him somewhat of a compliment. When he touched her skin, it was slightly sweaty but not hot or anything.

"Let me get you some water."

As he rushed to the kitchen, he swore if she didn't feel better in five minutes or so, he would be taking her ass to the ER.

"On your way back from the kitchen," she began huskily, "could you bring me some Twizzlers?"

And ... she's back.

Sal rolled his eyes heavenward, feeling foolish at himself for being so concerned with his snooping neighbor's wellbeing, which he had wished many weekends of her eviction or death. Whichever one came first.

"Where are they?" He didn't see them anywhere in the tiny old kitchen.

"In the candy drawer," she yelled back over the couch, sounding perfectly fine. "The one closest to the fridge."

"Of course, you have a fucking candy drawer," he muttered quietly under his breath as he tried opening it to find it stuffed to the brim with MoonPies and Nutty Buddies.

"I don't see any!" he called out again in frustration when its contents only held items mostly from that Little Debbie bitch.

"The drawer on the *other* side of the fridge!"

Already opening the other one, he found it, too, was stuffed but held items like Gummy Bears, Starbursts, and Snickers, along with her Twizzlers.

When he returned with the Twizzlers in hand, Valerie smiled.

"Sorry, that other one was my snack drawer."

THE LOONEY BIN

Valerie chewed on her Twizzlers, deep in thought. After showering and putting on some fresh clean clothes, she felt a lot better considering she was worth two million dollars. Sal hadn't left yet, still concerned she might pass out from her hot shower. She had half a mind to feel a little bit embarrassed about her tirade but, luckily for her, she no longer gave a fuck. Valerie had already experienced the most embarrassing moment in all her life when she'd gotten arrested, followed by her temper tantrum in the back of the cop car. It was hard to feel any embarrassment after that, not to mention she had already shown Sal her true imp self.

Taking another Twizzlers from the bag, she couldn't believe her predicament. How the hell was she supposed to find out who was framing her without her computer?

The phone ringing in Sal's pocket gave her a bright idea. She might not be able to use electronic devices ...

But Sal could.

He definitely wasn't as skilled as she was, *but I'm sure I could talk him through it.*

The hardest part was going to be the fact she was going to have to play nice with him for a little bit longer.

"I'll bring her in."

Catching the end of his phone call, Valerie grew worried. "Bring me in where?"

Sal gave her a smile. "That will ruin the surprise."

"I-I don't want to go back to jail."

When he saw the worry in her eyes, he let her know he had no plans of taking her there. "I wouldn't take you to jail. Besides, I'd get way too much enjoyment seeing you arrested again."

With her eyes turning to slits, any fear of being taken back to a cell were gone, knowing he would, in fact, love to see that again.

She was about to tell him to fuck off and kick rocks but had to remind herself that she needed him.

"Let's go." He motioned for her to move toward the front door.

"You're really not going to tell me where we're going?"

Sal shook his head. "Nope."

"Fine." She got up, rolling her eyes, and headed out with him. It wasn't like Salvatore Lastra was dangerous in any way, *right*? Officer Daniels' fear and warning of Sal entered her mind, but then she almost practically laughed. *Nah!* Hell, he wore glasses, for Christ's sake. Dangerous men didn't wear glasses.

When an image of Jeffery Dahmer popped into her brain with those big fugly glasses, she decided to actually go into her destroyed computer room and pick up her bat.

Sal giving her an incredulous look made her say, "Just in case you do get any ideas, 'cause so help me God, if you do take me to the police department"—Valerie gave the bat in her hands a flourishing twirl—"they'll be charging me with murder next."

Sal swallowed. "Good to know."

They walked out of the house; he headed for his Cadillac while she moved toward her car.

"Oh, and I'm driving. You can give me the directions as we go."

"No—"

"Do you want to go or not?" she asked, tossing the bat on her shoulder.

This time, it was his eyes rolling back at her stubbornness before he got something from the glovebox of his Cadillac that she couldn't make out before it disappeared in his suit jacket and headed toward the passenger side of her car. Obvious by the way he was looking at her 2005 Scion XB, he thought it was a shit box.

Smiling victoriously, she didn't care what he thought. Sal's car was more of an antique than hers.

She got in the car and placed her bat between the driver's side door and her left leg, out of his reach.

"Of course, you leave your keys in the ignition, too," he grumbled, finally getting in himself.

"Sure do," she said, starting the old box-looking car and relaxing. One thing was for certain: Sal was no Dahmer.

Dahmer never would have told a single woman not to leave their keys in the ignition or to find a better hiding spot for their key than under their front door mat.

As they journeyed on while she took his directions with somewhat difficulty, it didn't take long before the direction they were going seemed somewhat familiar to her.

"Right, not left!" he corrected in a rush when her wheels started turning the wrong direction. "And fucking slow down a bit."

Sal was clearly frustrated by now, and she didn't miss the curses under his breath, along with him saying, "How the hell do you play video games and don't know your lefts and rights?"

Letting his curses slide, she took a long stretch of road, wondering where the hell he was taking her. Then she immediately realized she had taken this way almost every day on her way ... to work.

Almost certain he was taking her to the Horseshoe, she couldn't understand one thing. *But why?*

"Pull over here."

"Here?"

"Yes, here!" he shouted exasperatingly with all patience lost.

Doing as he asked, she pulled over and put the car in *Park*. "Why are we going to the Horseshoe?"

Sal cleared his throat. "We're not."

Every hair on her body stood up in warning as she suddenly realized he wanted her to go to the place *across the street* from the Horseshoe.

The suit.

The Cadillac.

Lucca Caruso bailing her out.

Officer Daniels' warnings about Sal.

Holy fuck.

Valerie swallowed hard, wondering what her next move should be, knowing she was sitting right next to a made man. This whole time, her biggest enemy had been a glorified gangster, a legit mobster whom she had snooped on, cussed out, and to top it all off, ate Taco Bell in his car just to piss him off.

She desperately gripped the steering wheel, wanting to reach for the bat. She was stupidly brave, but she wasn't *that* stupidly brave. There was no winning in this situation. Sure, she could whack him before he whacked her, but then what? The mafia would send her a gutted fish before the morning came.

Understanding that she had put the puzzle pieces together after sensing her fear, he spoke in a calming tone. "No one's going to hurt you, Valerie. I promise."

With her gut betraying her, telling her to trust him, she figured it was his job to get people to trust him, and he was good at it. *Too good at it.*

"Lucca Caruso just wants to talk."

"L-*Lucca Caruso?*" she mouthed, almost unbelieving. When he confirmed with a nod, she licked her parched lips. "He's your boss, isn't he?"

"Yes."

Well, he didn't lie, at least.

Heart racing, she still held tightly to the wheel. She had been baiting a man who was most likely a dangerous individual, based off Officer Daniels' warnings that, in fact, weren't so baseless after all, making her realize she wasn't *stupidly brave.* She was just *stupid.*

"And"—she finally made herself look at him—"if I say no?"

He removed his glasses with a smile and placed them in the front pocket of his navy suit. "Come on, Valerie ..."

Her name coming off his lips no longer sounded lame. As she stared at him now without his glasses and his sly smile, he reminded her of a cunning fox.

"You're not even a little bit curious to meet the man who bailed you out of jail for two million dollars?"

Feeling cornered, she fought back the feeling, knowing he was right. She, in fact, did. Even though she was a thousand percent certain it would be the dumbest thing, *which was saying a lot*, she ever would do and without certainty would bite her in the ass. But, truth be told, getting whacked by Lucca Caruso didn't sound so bad, considering she was most likely facing life in prison. A girl like Valerie was never going to survive being locked up without going to the looney bin, anyway. Leaving her only option to take any and all help from the Boogieman himself ... and his sly minion.

"All right." Grabbing her bat, she exited the car with it in hand. "Let's go."

"You can't take that in," he scoffed, jumping out of the car to stop her before she could walk right in the front doors.

Valerie stopped to look at him. "Are you telling me you're not carrying a gun right now?"

Silence met her question. She had her answer.

"Then I should be able to carry a weapon myself," she said, pushing on ahead as Sal became frustrated again.

"Fucking hell, Valerie."

However, mistaking him as just her annoying neighbor wasn't going to happen again, not after seeing him for what he truly was.

Entering the Casino Hotel felt like entering the fox's den. She just hoped she wouldn't become his prey.

The concerned glances she got from those gambling in the casino had security on their tail in no time. Only the fact that Sal stood beside her was the reason she was able to proceed all the way to the elevators.

Waiting on the doors to open, she expected one of the many security guards who had accumulated to stop them.

The fact they got in and watched the doors close them inside still without interference as Sal hit a series of buttons told her one thing.

Salvatore was a made man who must be pretty damn close to the top.

She couldn't help but give him a hard look, wondering how it was possible to misjudge him so horribly all this time.

"Do you even need glasses?" she asked in disbelief.

Sal didn't answer, clearly preferring to ride the elevator in silence.

Her eyes made their way down to his suit and shiny expensive shoes. "You're freaking rich, too, aren't you?"

Again, no answer, causing her to practically blow a bubble with a huff of air. "Of course, you are. The car you drive is probably just another layer to your *façade* that you belong like the rest of us, living paycheck to paycheck on Prairie Drive. What a joke ..." She laughed at herself. "I bet you wouldn't know what it was like to scrape by a day in your life."

Those words had Sal hitting another series of buttons that sent the elevator to a screeching halt on its long ascent to the top.

"What is your problem?"

"*My problem?*" she asked incredulously.

"Yes." He stealthily stalked closer to her with black fury in his eyes. "What is *your* fucking problem? You've hated me since the day I moved in next door."

Valerie gasped. "I did not!"

"Oh, please, Valerie. You've had it out for me since then, and you know it. I'll never forget seeing your beady little eyes snooping through my window that first night." With each word, he stepped closer and closer to her.

"My eyes are not beady!" she gasped even louder, in greater offense. Taking her bat, she lifted it, pointing the end right at his chest. "I only started snooping when *what I thought was your girlfriend, by the way,* came home because I thought she was *way* out of your league." She had let the bat fall to his chest, forcing him back to the corner of the elevator. "I didn't have it out for you till you showed up two weeks later with a different girl. That's when I started to hate you."

Sal only looked at her like she was crazier than she already was. "And *why* did that make you hate me, exactly?"

She began hitting the buttons that he had hit when they'd first entered. "Because only the worst kind of cheater would get a house just to bang a different chick every other weekend. I bet you live on the rich part of town. huh? What? You got a wife and possibly a kid? Or just a long-term girlfriend whose little heart you can't seem to break?"

SHE FUCKING THINKS WHAT?

Pinching the bridge of his nose for dear life while the elevator restarted its ascent, he was afraid he might hurt a woman for the first time in his life if he let go. All this time, Valerie hated him because she thought he was a cheater?

"Christ, Valerie," was all he could manage to say before he finally got a hold of himself. The woman even had the audacity to point out she had memorized the code that would continue their trip to the top uninterrupted.

His jaw flexed over and over again until the elevator came to its stop and the doors swung open. He stayed in place, letting her go first, deciding to finally speak only as she passed him.

"I'm not a cheater."

"Yeah, sure, buddy," she sarcastically agreed with a pat to his back before she disappeared off the elevator.

Looking heavenward, he spoke to the Big Man upstairs, hoping to bypass a confession in his near future.

I'm going to kill her if You don't.

THE BOOGIEMAN AND HIS SLY MINION

"Come in, Ms. Monroe."

Chills coated her body from just his voice alone, still sight unseen. She had been given the pleasure of never having seen the man claimed as the Boogieman in her life, even though she had worked across the street from him for six months. Now, only a door separated them, and she was called upon by name.

Having only "heard" of him was probably what scared her the most. She hoped putting a face to the name might humanize him, make him less frightening.

It was like the final boss fight in a video game; you feared getting to the end of the story and not being ready to battle them, but it turned out, most of the time, they looked ridiculous, and you had nothing to fear after all. However, that wasn't the case when Sal revealed what was behind the door.

It was a large office with tall windows showcasing the beauty of Kansas City from this vantage point. An oversized wooden desk sat in the room, and behind it sat an impending man with eyes that complemented the city lights down below. With one look, he gave you a good reason to fear him. He sent any goose bumps she had into a frozen frost, so much so that Sal had to push her forward and into his office with a firm hand on her back, and then she was finally in the presence of the Boogieman and his sly minion.

"Hello, Ms. Monroe," the Caruso boss greeted her coldly, only further giving her a reason to fear him.

The worst part about him, though? It was his looks. Devilishly handsome. As a woman, it made you want to reach out and touch him to see if he was real, but your instincts fought every ounce of that, knowing who he truly was. He was frightening and beautiful at the same time, making him hold up to the name of being the most dangerous man in all of Kansas City.

His blue-green eyes that were simply terrifying traveled down to the object in her hands. "Is there a reason you're carrying a bat through my Casino Hotel?"

Nervously grasping it in both hands, she didn't know how to tell him it was because she knew exactly who he was and the kind of establishment she was coming into.

"I see." Lucca nodded, seeing the hidden answer. "Please, sit."

It was hard not to obey what sounded like an order from him, so she slowly took one of the two chairs in front of his desk before he continued.

"You are aware of who I am, then?"

Valerie nodded, both of them knowing it wasn't just his surname he was insinuating.

"Well, it was either very brave of you to bring in a weapon ... or stupid."

Unfortunately, she agreed, and hearing the word *brave* finally made her enough so to speak.

"I suppose so."

Leaning back in his chair, he studied her for a moment. "Something tells me you are not stupid, Ms. Monroe."

"Valerie," she offered. "You can call me Valerie. I think bailing me out for two million dollars gives you that right."

A smile tilted his lips for a mere second, and she wasn't sure she liked it. She much preferred him without the deadly smile. It somehow made him even better-looking, and that wasn't something she wanted to think.

"I suppose it should," he agreed before picking up a pack of cigarettes and lifting them. "Do you mind?"

"Not at all." She waved her hand slightly, hoping he'd blow the nicotine in her direction to calm her nerves.

When he lit the glorious end up, she contemplated asking the Boogieman for one herself.

Relaxing into his chair from the first hit, he got back to her earlier point. "Do you know *why* I bailed you out?"

"Trust me, Mr. Carus—"

"Lucca," he offered back with a puff of smoke. "I think we're both entitled to a first-name basis."

"All right." She cleared her throat, starting again, "Trust me, *Lucca*; I wouldn't have come here to find out if I did." Again, it was another thing she didn't like. Using his first name. It humanized him.

He tapped some ashes off his cigarette into a crystal ash tray. "I understand you worked for the Horseshoe?"

"That's correct."

"Well, despite the claims being made against you by your previous employer, Sal claims you to be innocent."

Her head suddenly snapped back to look at Sal over her shoulder, to see him standing in the far corner of the room. She had almost forgotten about him—he had been so quiet.

"Is that so?" she gritted out, giving him a dirty look.

"Frankly, Valerie—"

Her name out of the Boogieman's mouth sent another set of frost across her skin as she turned back to face him.

"I couldn't care less if you *were* the one who cyber attacked the Horseshoe, but if you did, I need to know now so we know how to proceed. Mr. Bryant is a great attorney, and I'm sure he's more than—"

"Oh, I'm innocent." She decided to save him the time of explaining. "You don't have to worry about that."

"That's good, then." Lucca fully believed her, taking another puff of his cigarette and blowing out the smoke, filling the room. "Do you know who possibly did and why they would want to frame you?"

She slumped her shoulders. It was the question she'd had on her brain since the moment the cuffs had been slid around her wrists. "I have no idea."

"All right, then. Tell us everything you talked about with the lawyer, as well as anything that stuck out to you while working there."

Valerie was detailed, replaying everything she'd said to Kent, as well as her time working at the Horseshoe, including the date she'd started and the date she'd been fired, along with everything in between. All the while, Lucca smoked cigarette after cigarette until it was Sal who sat in the chair as she went from pacing to touching things in the office, finally inching closer and closer to Lucca's desk.

"Do you mind blowing the smoke in this direction?" she asked, waving the nicotine goodness toward her.

That was when Lucca respectively put his cigarette out. "I think we've heard enough for now. Thank you, Valerie."

"No problem at all," she assured him and let her inner thoughts take over by going for the pack of cigarettes on his desk, but a cold hand came out to stop her.

"You may take your seat again."

Snatching her hand back in shock, she took the chair next to a smirking Sal, feeling awkward. After getting lost in the details, *and her cravings*, she had become comfortable enough to forget whose presence she was in.

Letting her speak uninterrupted for quite some time, the mob boss now began his questioning.

"Have you been able to find employment yet?"

She cleared her throat. "Not yet. But I've been lookin—"

"Don't bother," he said with a wave of his hand. "Sal will find a position for you here at the Casino Hotel." He looked over at him. "Won't you?"

Sal quickly sat up straight. "S-Sure."

"And since I have such a sizable investment placed on you, Valerie"—Lucca glanced between the both of them—"I hope you don't mind that Sal will follow your every move to ensure you are where you need to be?"

Both Valerie and Sal stood up from their chairs and spoke in loud unison, *"What?"*

"Do you mind giving us a minute?" Lucca asked, looking at just her.

"Sure," Valerie said with a grumble, moving toward the door. She went for her bat that she had set beside the door during her speech, but he stopped her with a hand held up.

"That's far enough," he said, crossing around the desk so he and Sal could speak in hushed tones.

"I'll wait, then." She turned her back to them; it was only then that she felt safe enough to roll her eyes in front of Lucca.

In a desperate attempt to listen to them, she strained her ears. She could almost believe they sounded like brothers ... bickering.

"I'm not fucking babysitting her crazy ass any longer!" Sal began in an aggressively hushed tone. "Give her over to Amo. I'm sure he'd love this psycho."

Lucca sat on the edge of his desk with a shit-eating grin. "Nah, I don't think so. It's your turn to do some grunt work for a change."

"No. No. No fucking way. I didn't learn to use my brain and sit behind a computer all day to do this. I did it to *avoid* instances like this."

"And that's why you're perfect for this job, brother," Lucca said, hitting his shoulder. "Who else in the family is capable to help her figure out who attacked the Horseshoe? Do you really think Amo, or anyone else for that matter, is going to be able to do that? I doubt my other men know the difference between a monitor and a computer."

"Well, see, you do," Sal huffed, hoping he might still be able to get out of this death sentence.

"Well, I'm not a fucking idiot," Lucca told him. "My other men are useful for other things, but using their brains isn't one. Why do you think I have yet to pick an underboss?"

Fuck! Lucca was right, and he knew it. It was a position Sal probably would have had, if the job he already did for Lucca wasn't so important. His friend would eventually find an underboss who could handle the job in a few years, but replacing Sal would be impossible. Lucca already bent the family rules for his sister Maria to be his consigliere—that's how little options he had currently in the family.

"Yeah, yeah, whatever."

"So, you'll do it, then ...?"

Sal ran a rough hand through his hair. "I mean, are you asking or telling me, Lucca?"

Lucca gave him a sympathetic look. "I told you long ago I'd never ask you to do anything for me you didn't want to do, and I meant it. We're brothers. Our bond is stronger than my brothers whom I share blood with, and you know I haven't even given Nero a promise like that. In fact, I purposefully give him the shitty jobs. Plus, are you really going to let an innocent woman go down for this?"

Ugh. Sal hated when Lucca pulled that card, even though he was truthful in the fact he wouldn't make him do anything he didn't want. But how was he supposed to say no after a speech like that?

"Fine, I'll do it," he finally agreed while making one thing clear. However, it was uncertain if he was making it clear to Lucca or himself. "But only for you, not for her."

"Damn." He couldn't believe the savage statement. "You don't care if she ends up in prison? That's harsh for you."

"Nope." Sal shook his head violently. "I have practically dreamed of her going to prison every single night I spent in my home."

"Really?" Surprised at his deep distaste for her, Lucca peered over at the woman in question. "Did you look her up and find something?"

Even though he hated to admit it ... "No, she's clean. Her search history is boringly PG, unlike the video games she plays. The only things against her are some parking and speeding tickets. She's also behind a couple of months on her mortgage payments and bills, but I'm sure she is considering she was recently fired, not like we care about that stuff, anyway."

"So, what's the issue?" Lucca asked, looking back at

him. "I've only seen you act like this if you know they've done something rancid."

It was scary to wield the power to know about a person's full digital Internet history. It was like being able to read people's minds or know a person's deepest, darkest secret. It regretfully made you weary of people and have an aversion to humans. Eventually, he had to quit looking so deeply into any woman he came into contact with who he found attractive; otherwise, he would never ever get laid.

"You really have to ask?" he said, looking back at her with her bat back in her hand.

Lucca's voice went even lower as he stared at the girl in concern. "What's wrong with her?"

"She plays video games too much."

"Ah ..." He nodded, getting it now. It was clear that was all Lucca needed to hear to understand her.

"Yeah, so, imagine living next door to that!" Sal quipped, losing his cool.

"Shh ..." Lucca reminded him with a laugh. "So, she's *eccentric*. So, what?"

"If by eccentric you mean *certifiable*, sure."

"Do yourself a favor and look around here. We're all certifiable, Sal," Lucca told him, knowing it was the truth. Every made man was a psychotic individual, held on by a tight leash that the craziest one of all controlled. They were only one bad day away from Lucca Caruso and the whole family crashing down.

Smiling, his boss and friend looked over at her once more, and Sal really didn't like the look of his shit-eating grin.

"Something tells me she'll fit right in."

$$\infty$$

"It's settled," Lucca spoke up again to finally include her in the no-longer-private conversation. "You'll stay with Sal at his place here in the Casino Hotel until further notice."

What?

"Listen, I, uh ... really don't think that's a good idea." She crossed the room closer to him. At this point, she thought she preferred prison rather than living with Salvatore.

However, Lucca's patience had finally been worn thin. "And I really don't car—"

"But isn't he married?"

"Excuse me?" Lucca asked her in disbelief while Sal put his face in his palm.

"Isn't Sal married?" she asked again, more clearly. "I just really don't think it would be appropriate if I stayed with him. I promise not to run or anything. Maybe you have an extra room I could use here—"

Lucca held up his hand, silencing her. "I can assure you, Valerie, Sal is not married."

"Oh." Valerie didn't know why a part of her felt happy at that fact, but there was the question of ... "Well, maybe he has a girlfriend?"

Another smile touched Lucca's lips, this time lingering longer. "That, I do not keep track of, but you will still be under his supervision and staying with him."

When she went to protest again, it was Sal who stopped her from arguing by nudging her along.

Knowing she had pressed her luck too far on that subject, she still dared to ask a different question. "Can I at least keep my bat?"

Lucca's deadly smile continued as he looked over at Sal and said, "Be my guest."

Wow. This might be better than prison after all—

"Oh, and, Valerie," Lucca said, stopping them before they left, "you have my full permission to use it on any of my men that you see fit."

Way better than prison.

But before the door could close, he finally spared one of his men.

"Anyone but Sal."

Damn, you can't win 'em all.

CHIN UP

Valerie wasn't sure what to expect before Sal opened the door to his penthouse. The city lights glowed through the floor-to-ceiling windows and highlighted his decor. While the luxuriousness of the space was over the top, his furniture was understated with warm neutrals and touches of navy-blue hues. It was truly breathtaking and yet somehow felt like home for a space that should feel a bit pretentious.

In disbelief at the sight, she barely could get her words out. "A-And you live *here*?"

Shutting the door behind him, he nodded. "Yes."

"This is *nice*." Clearly finding her voice, she dropped her bat and made herself right at home by throwing herself down on the lush couch. She felt the luxe material, thinking she could get used to this. The futon she had been sleeping on, she wasn't sure she could go back to after a night on this bad boy.

Looking back over at Sal, she could see he fit in his surroundings here better. How she hadn't noticed he didn't belong on Prairie Drive sooner, she would never understand. It was like witnessing the difference between Clark Kent and Superman in real life. It wasn't just the glasses that made all the difference; it was the personality—no, the *confidence.*

Every piece of new information about him made him more enigmatic to her, and she needed to know more. The real question, however, was: Clark Kent hid who he was because of his powers ...

So, what *is Salvatore hiding?*

"Do all the men who work for Lucca get a room at the Casino Hotel, or just you?"

The nonchalant way she tried to play it off didn't work. Sal could see her curiosity behind her eyes, while behind his, he contemplated what he could or couldn't reveal.

"Come on." She gave him a knowing look. "I think it's safe to say the rumors about the Carusos are true. I've seen behind the proverbial curtain, but don't worry, because we both know it would do me zero favors to ever spill the beans. Plus, I have absolutely no one to tell. I have no friends. Well, that's not true. I have one friend."

Sal laughed mockingly. "Who? Your *huge* boyfriend?"

"Okay, fine, so I lied about having a boyfriend. Sue me." She shrugged the lie off quickly. "They're just a friend I've been playing games with online for a couple of years now."

Shaking his head at her, he let the big fat lie slide, considering he'd known it was bullshit, anyway. He found himself taking the chair next to the couch to ask her a question with his curiosity piqued, though he chalked that curiosity up to deciding what he should or shouldn't reveal to her about the family. "No family?"

"Welp, my mom left to go get a pack of cigarettes, but that was when I was two—"

"Ouch." Sal couldn't help but feel that pain for her.

"Then there's my father." She adjusted, making herself more comfortable on his sofa as she freely started to over-share. "I have to give him credit for at least *trying* to stick around for me at that age. But, you know, it was hard for him to raise a kid, and a daughter at that, alone, so he married another woman pretty quickly after my mother left. My stepmother was nice in the beginning, but I noticed the older I got, the more she started to begrudge me for spending more time with my dad as he got me into computers and video games. She made sure to dig a wedge right into us before I turned eighteen and forced him to choose between me or her after I graduated high school. And since I was going off to college, I think he was scared of the thought of being alone again, so he decided I was the one to cut off."

Double ouch. While Sal couldn't relate much to that part of her story, he supposed there was the perk of his father never wanting him to begin with. "I'm sorry about your jealous bitch of a stepmother."

"It's okay. I guess I should be thankful she at least waited till I could go live in a dorm to do it, so I wouldn't be homeless."

Swallowing hard, Sal was grateful not to have to comment as she continued speaking.

"My father's the one who I really blame. She didn't technically owe me anything. We weren't blood related or anything, you know?"

That statement made his body seethe for Valerie.

"No, you weren't. And while I agree your father is a piece of shit, she's no less of a piece of shit than he is. Whether you're related to someone by blood or not is irrelevant. The day she married your father was the day she chose to accept you as family as well, considering you were only a child. If anything, she should have encouraged your relationship with your father and, even more importantly, your interests and talent. I'm sorry, Valerie, but none of your family was your true family."

"I guess I never thought about it that way." Those words quietly left her lips in sadness but also realization.

A few quiet moments in contemplation passed before she spoke again.

"You know, it sounds like you're speaking from experience. Is that how you ended up becoming loyal to the Carusos?"

"How I got where I am today is rather complicated and a long story that will put you to sleep considering how tired you must be."

"Oh, I doubt that," she said, highly interested, but it wasn't hard to miss the heavy lids growing, her eyes looking wearier by the second.

"You can take my room upstairs, if you'd like," he offered, but there would be no answer as she had fallen fast asleep after her eventful weekend and day.

Not bothering to move her, considering how comfortable she looked, he went upstairs to grab a few things before coming back down.

Placing one of his shirts on the couch beside her, he did so in case she woke up in the middle of the night and wanted to be more comfortable, before he covered her with a cozy blanket. Tomorrow, he would have to figure out a way to get some of her stuff here for the time being.

Despite wanting to curse Lucca for forcing his hand to help her, his feelings of strong *hate* toward her were slowly turning into strong *dislike*.

Unable to help himself, he brushed some of the silky hair off her face with his fingertips to reveal more of her sunlit kisses.

Fine. Mild *dislike.*

"Good night, Valerie." Sal finally pulled himself away from her to catch some sleep as well. "Sweet dreams."

It was going to be something he instinctively knew he wasn't going to have tonight ...

IT WAS SAL'S TENTH BIRTHDAY AND HAD BEEN GOING pretty shitty until he noticed his mother waving him down after the school bell rang.

To say school was fun when you were homeless would be a stretch of the imagination. Him being so advanced for his age only made it that much worse.

"You like it?" His mother wiggled her brows at her son playfully.

It took Sal a minute to figure out she was talking about the navy-colored car she was standing in front of.

"It's a Cadillac Coupe de Ville," she said proudly. "For your birthday."

"What?" his child mind said in disbelief before they both jumped into the car. "This is so cool!" He knew it wasn't new by any means, but it still felt like a spaceship to him, considering they had never owned a car before in his whole life. "Wow!" He ran his young hand across the dash. "I love it. How'd you get it?"

"I won it," she said, flashing a broken smile.

That, Sal highly doubted.

Ruffling his chestnut hair, she started the car up, making his smile brighter. "How was school?"

Slowly, his smile disappeared. "It was okay."

"The kids are just jealous of how smart you are, honey. Don't you worry; everything's going to be different now. We have this car we can sleep in, so no more shelter, and I'm about to come into some money, so we can finally buy a house on the upper side. That way, you can start going to school with kids who are more your speed."

For his mother's sake, Sal faked a smile and nodded his head, knowing that was never, ever going to happen. Every time she got better, it only lasted for a month or two before they were right back on the streets. While it was the first car she had ever gotten, he knew it wasn't going to last.

Of course, he wasn't wrong about it not lasting forever, but it did at least last longer than he'd originally thought before his spaceship was swooped up by a tow truck.

Those had been the happiest four months of his life, and one day, he swore he'd get one just like it for them again when he was older.

The day it was taken away had been hard. It had been so cold, wet, and rainy all day for them not to have a roof over their heads, and he knew the night was only going to be rougher. To top it all off, he was starving.

Hearing his stomach growl, she reached into her pocket to come out with only two dollars. "It's okay, honey. We'll make do. Come on."

When cash was this low, there was only one place they could go and both eat.

Taco Bell.

You could get a burrito for less than a dollar; it being filled with rice and beans did a good job filling them up for the day so they wouldn't go too hungry.

Entering the fast food place, he figured his mom planned on halving the burrito since she only ordered one. She probably wanted to save the rest of the two bucks for their next meal, since their luck had been so low lately.

He opened the food up from its packaging, but she stopped him before he could break it in half.

"No, thanks, honey. You eat it. I'm not hungry."

Sal couldn't help but notice her scratching her arms and the shivering, despite them finally not being out in the cold. It was hard to stomach the food, considering it was their fifth night eating Taco Bell, yet you always were to finish your food if you weren't sure where your next meal would come from.

The two stretched the time before they had to go back out into the cold for as long as they could until a worker finally came and told them it was time for them to leave.

His mother never went without a few curses, but Sal managed to get her to leave by pulling her out the door before he got too embarrassed, or worse—they could never return. Truthfully, Sal couldn't have cared less if he didn't get to eat at this shithole for the rest of his life, but it was better than starving to death.

As they left the restaurant, he had an eerie feeling about what his mother was going to say before she said it—she always looked like this before she needed her next fix.

"Listen, honey, I need to go take care of a few thi—"

"But it's a full moon tonight," he exclaimed in a hurry after looking up at the sky.

"It's okay, honey. I'll be fine; don't worry," his mother

assured him. "I need to go do something to help get our apartment. Take this. Hopefully, it'll give you a few hours of playtime on the computer, then we'll meet up at our usual spot in three hours."

Sal looked at the outstretched change remaining from the money left. He didn't want to take it, but she forced him to, putting it in his pocket before giving him a big hug.

"I love you, honey."

"Love you, too, Mom."

She kissed him on his head. "See you in three hours."

Though he knew it was wrong to let her go, he did. It was always on a full moon night that Sal worried for his mom's sake. Usually, he could talk her into staying with him, afraid her stupid family superstition was true. But, for some reason, this night, he didn't. So, when he went to Terry's Internet café, he couldn't concentrate, finding himself looking out the window at the moon. The bad feeling in his stomach only made him sicker the longer the night went on. If he knew where she'd be, he'd go out looking for her, but he was supposed to wait until the clock struck midnight before he left.

Unable to wait any longer, he left five minutes early with dread overtaking his young body. A sigh of relief escaped him when he saw her walking toward him under the streetlamp glow. Little did he know, leaving those five minutes early that night was the only reason he was going to talk to her for the last time.

"Mom!" Sal cried as he ran toward her, closing the distance when she faltered, holding her stomach.

With her falling into his arms, they dropped to the pavement together. Trying to apply pressure where the blood flowed freely, he sobbed as tears streamed down his cheeks.

"Mom ..."

A tear slipped out of her own eyes, knowing her fate was sealed. "Oh, look how beautiful." Reaching out to take her son's face in her shaky hand, she pointed his tiny chin up so he'd look toward the night sky while her eyes never left him. "Chin up, honey. It's a full moon tonight."

DESPERATE TIMES CALL FOR
DESPERATE MEASURES

Sal woke up from the horrid, haunting memory, sweating profusely.

At ten years old, he had to understand that a drug deal gone bad was the reason he'd watched his mother bleed out on the pavement. He had lain there, holding her in his arms, crying out for help until his voice gave out. Not one person came to help him until the full moon began to disappear.

It was Dante who had found him.

Ever since Dante had seen him in the Internet café, he would drop by from time to time to check in on him. Upon his first look of Sal, he'd known that the child was Lucifer's son, and it didn't take him long to realize he was gifted beyond measure.

That early morning, as Dante headed to the café, dumb luck had him stumbling onto the scene. Afraid his adversary, Lucifer, would find out Sal was his child and groom him for himself now that his mother was gone, Dante did everything in his power to try to convince a young Sal to come live with him and his family. It wouldn't be until Sal turned thirteen on his birthday and had to eat Taco Bell out of the dumpster for the last time that Sal finally gave in. Having been told the truth by Dante of who his father was upon his return, he no longer desired to leave the Caruso family home and began to accept his mother's death and new family into his heart.

Sal's gifts made Dante prouder and prouder each day as they grew, so while Dante took him off the streets for selfish reasons, Sal became a true son to him, regardless of his parentage, having actually gotten closer to him as a father than his own sons he had fathered.

Dante's legitimate children, Lucca, Maria, Nero, and Leo, could have begrudged him for that fact. However, they never did. Each one accepted him into their family with open arms. They were a family not born out of blood but out of loyalty. A loyalty so strong that each of them would pay with blood.

It took him standing under a hot shower for a long time to finally calm. By the time he got back into bed, he couldn't help but hear a persistent thudding noise coming from downstairs.

Tossing the covers off him in a huff of air, he threw on his white sleeveless undershirt and patted down the steps to find her looking through his kitchen cabinets, opening and closing each one as if it wasn't the middle of the night.

"What on earth are you doing?" he growled from behind her with his arms crossed.

Half scared to death by his unknown presence, she jumped ten feet in the air.

Sal had no fucking idea how the girl could ever be good at video games; her awareness of her surroundings in real life was at a zero. How she'd made it to this age still alive, not kidnapped, or headless, he didn't understand.

"Fucking hell, you scared me half to death."

Under his breath, he mumbled, "Not like that's hard."

After finally calming her heart rate, she made a worried face. "I'm sorry, did I wake you? I thought I heard the shower running, so I decided it was safe to get up 'cause I'm starving."

How she was so small was another thing he'd never understand. Valerie had found the old shirt he'd left out for her, revealing more of her shape than her usual baggy attire. While it swallowed her in height, it fell against her tiny hourglass frame, and it slightly bothered him that he noticed.

"You didn't," he agreed, not wanting her to feel *too* bad. Taking a seat at the counter, he ran a ragged hand through his hair.

"Bad dream?" Valerie asked.

"Yeah, something like that."

After listening to her abuse another one of his cabinets, he finally gave up and got up from his seat to move toward a door that didn't really look like one since it blended into a cabinet seamlessly and revealed a secret pantry.

Her eyes grew in wonder. "No wonder I couldn't find any of the good shit!" After contemplating her options for a few minutes, it was obvious she still couldn't find what she wanted. "Have you ever heard of MSGs? Where do you shop? *Whole Foods*?"

Internally groaning, he leaned over her frame from behind her, causing him to internally groan for another reason. Grabbing a bag from the top shelf that she probably couldn't see, he held it out for her. "Try these."

When she wrinkled her nose, he found the action kind of cute as she sniffed the opened bag of cheese puffs that were, in fact, organic. Reaching in the perfectly small-portioned bag, she popped one in her mouth. "Not bad," Valerie said, going for another.

"Glad you like them," he commented, already heading back upstairs. Sal didn't trust himself this close to her so late at night in just a shirt if he found the action of her eating a cheese puff attractive.

The night he'd spent with Samantha had been so unsatisfactory. Sal wanted to blame Valerie for working himself up in anger and not being able to perform, but he was starting to realize that the truth was, Samantha wasn't the girl he had wanted that night.

There was no one on this Earth that made Sal as hard as he was right now, except the unbearable, aggravating woman standing in front of him.

"Wait," she said, causing him to curse internally.

Fuck. Fuck. Fuck. Fuck. Fuck. Christ, even her potty mouth was rubbing off on him.

"You don't happen to have any video games, do you? I'm usually wide awake at this time, working on my game or playing. I'm a night owl," she politely added, stating the obvious.

He nodded before going up to his bedroom, and she annoyingly followed behind.

"You don't mind, do you?"

Sal flexed his jaw. "Guess not."

Seeing the loft-like bedroom upstairs, then the huge walk-in closet, she couldn't help but appreciate the amenities. "Damn, it just keeps getting better and better."

Going to the back of his closet, he pulled out an old storage tub that, when he opened it, sent dust particles flying. Inside were all the old video games he and Terry used to play when he was a kid at the Internet café. It was a box of memories he hadn't opened since the day he'd placed the items in there. After his haunting dream, it gave him a bittersweet feeling to see them again.

"A Nintendo 64!" Valerie squealed, grabbing the system up carefully, along with the controllers.

He could instantly tell she looked at it the same way he did—with bittersweet memories of her own.

"I'm jealous you kept yours. I had to sell mine after I got kicked out of my home."

Sal felt for the poor girl, knowing if it weren't for Terry, he wouldn't have had a single thing from his childhood. While the car he drove was the Coupe de Ville his mom had owned for that short period of time, he knew it wasn't the exact one as the original that had gotten impounded. There was just something about still owning the original you had as a child that made the nostalgia of something so much better.

"Oh my God, you have Mario Kart for it, too," she gasped, catching sight of the game in the bottom of the tub. "I could kick anyone's ass on Rainbow Road."

Sal couldn't help but let his inner child take that as a threat. "Wanna bet?"

VALERIE HAD OFFICIALLY DIED AND GONE TO HEAVEN.

Here she was, in a sick-ass penthouse that overlooked the city, with a man who looked hot as hell right about now as he began plugging the old gaming system into the TV, *and* she was about to play Nintendo 64? This was a gamer girl's fantasy.

If this was what the mafia was like, she wanted to sign on the dotted line. Even if she had to do it in blood, she didn't give a fuck. This was great! Going to jail was the best thing that had ever happened to her in all her life!

"Does the mafia accept women?"

Sal stopped what he was doing for a moment, clearly taken aback by her bluntness.

DOES SHE WANT TO DIE?

Never in all his life had an outsider asked him something like that, let alone just come out and say the word *mafia*. He knew she understood how serious it was, considering she had brought a weapon in to meet the head of the family, yet she'd say risky shit like that?

The woman was an anomaly, for sure, and she was damn fucking lucky he was the one who controlled all the cameras and audio in the Casino Hotel. God forbid Lucca heard her talk so freely.

The question was: Did he entertain it in private? Should he just shut her ass down here and now? Or did he just say fuck it, 'cause the woman wasn't stupid enough to believe anything other than the truth, anyways?

Goddammit ... Lucca's going to kick my fucking as—

"NOT *EXACTLY*."

"Well, what does *not exactly* mean?" she asked. Sensing Sal's frustration with the wires, she went to help him hook it up correctly. When she took a look, it was no wonder he was having trouble—he had all the wires messed up.

What a noob.

Flustered from her questioning, Sal gave up and let her do it. He knew exactly how to hook the stupid thing up. He had only done it a million times growing up. He was The Great fucking Salvatore, for fuck's sake. If she knew he was the notorious hacker, there was no way Valerie would have even stepped in to help in the first place. Knowing her degree and job, he knew without a shadow of a doubt Valerie knew *of* The Great Salvatore, but he had yet to tell her, secretly hoping it would never come out. If he thought she talked too much now, he would never get her to shut up if she did know exactly who he was. All the questions she'd ask him about how he did this or that would be endless. This whole time, Valerie was thinking he was hiding only the fact he was a made man, when in actuality, little did she know he was more concerned with hiding his even bigger secret.

"Come on ..." Valerie nudged, looking like she was about to resort to begging. "I promise I won't tell anyone. I haven't even been able to contact my friend." You could see something click in her mind, then. "Shit, he's probably worried sick, actually. I'll need to find a way to talk to him—"

"*Him?*" an astonished Sal questioned once he realized her sole friend, whom she had been playing with for years, was a guy. For some reason, albeit sexist, he'd assumed Valerie played online with a girl when she mentioned her friend.

"Yes ..." She stared at him strangely and like he'd suddenly grown a third eye. "Justice is a guy. Why would that matter?"

Shit, am I jealous?

"No reason," he quickly clarified, but his words were unable to convince even himself. The stinge of jealousy was unprecedented for him and simply couldn't go unnoticed.

Sighing, he took a seat on the edge of his bed in defeat from needing his thoughts and this conversation to move on to a different subject. So much so, he was even willing to risk his own life to do so—

"LATELY, IT'S BEEN COMPLICATED. *BEFORE* LUCCA TOOK over the family, no woman had ever been anywhere near the business. But recently, the first one in Caruso history took a position."

"*Ooo* ... that's so cool." Proud the family had stepped into the twenty-first century, she was slightly envious, but way more intrigued of the mystery lady. "I need to meet her."

"Oh no, you don't." He nipped that right in the bud. "I will be doing everything in my power to make sure you don't meet Maria."

Valerie pouted. "You're no fun."

"I will, however, be letting you meet my sister, Katarina. While she's not as heavily into the family business as Maria is, she is married to a made man and has taken on an accounting role. I think she might have a job for you at the Casino Hotel."

"Don't get me wrong or anything—I'm excited to meet your sister—but I'm not that good with numbers. I'd rather vomit every day for the rest of my life than do anything with accounting."

"I'm confident, between my sister and I, we will find something for you here."

For some reason, Valerie really didn't like the sound of that. But she'd worry about that at a later time. Right now, as she got the old gaming system finally up and running, it was time to whoop Sal's ass in Mario Kart.

"You sure you want to hook it up in your bedroom?" she asked a bit nervously when it was time to sit down beside him on the bed, since there was no chair. The way he looked in his tight, sleeveless shirt as it showed off his lean muscles was simply criminal.

"The TV downstairs doesn't have the right hookup. It's too new."

Lies.

Liar.

Big fucking liar.

The system could so hook up to the TV downstairs, but he didn't have any other perfectly good reason to get her in his bed. Other than being honest with the fact he wanted to fuck her ... and *that* he didn't even want to admit to himself, as she had been his sworn enemy for the past six months.

What a sad life he was beginning to live. Never in his life had he had to use video games to sleep with a woman, which was quite shocking considering who he was.

Fuck. Am I that desperate that I've had to resort to these measures?

When Valerie had to step past him to sit down on the edge of the bed beside him, she gave him her back, thinking that was the better way to squeeze by, but since he was leaning forward a bit with his hands between his knees, his knuckles grazed the soft skin of her legs, and he got a full view of her ass covered by his shirt.

Swallowing hard, he found himself awfully thirsty. *Desperate times call for desperate measures ...*

"I'm hot," Sal announced before lazily taking his shirt off. "Are you hot?"

Holy fuck. Hell yeah, you are ... she couldn't help but think after getting a glorious look at his tanned back.

As he pulled the material over his head, the action had flexed his back muscles, revealing that he wasn't that lean after all. His thick suits had just hidden all the goods.

Licking her suddenly dry lips, she tried to get a hold of herself. "N-Now that you mention it, I could use some water."

"Be right back," he said, getting up to head downstairs.

The bed having released some weight rose quite a bit, showing he weighed more than she'd thought, too.

Unable to keep herself from gawking, she watched his back and every muscle he had like a hawk until he disappeared down the steps.

"Fuck! Fuck! Fuckity fuck!" Valerie whispered harshly for only her ears.

And she had Cheeto Puff breath. *Great.*

She tried to desperately reprimand herself for having thoughts of kissing him; she didn't want herself getting any more ideas.

"He has a girlfriend! I know he has to. Hell, he probably has three! Just look at him—"

Her voice quietly trailed off when the front side of him came back into view from up the steps. His backside had nothing on the front. Those hint of abs dipping into his low-waisted gray sweatpants should be a fucking crime.

God ... please forgive me.

BY THE TIME SAL MADE IT BACK UPSTAIRS, HE THOUGHT he had control of himself.

Keyword: *thought.*

All that silly self-control was gone when he caught sight of her eyes slowly moving lower down his body.

There was no woman on Earth who had resisted him after that move. Was taking off his shirt pathetic? *Yes.* But it worked a hundred percent of the time, every time.

He held out the fresh glass of water; he had actually downed a glass himself downstairs real quick, and now he could see the thirst on her lips.

Hook. Line. And sinker.

RENDERING VALERIE SPEECHLESS

Taking the offered water, she desperately began drinking the contents, swishing it a bit in her mouth while he went through the menu of the game.

Sal was right; it was scorching in here. He'd brought her one measly glass of cold water when she needed a fire hose to put out the flames he was raising in her body.

Scooting into a more comfortable position, she rested her back against the headboard, then pulled her legs together in a lotus position that she had learned when she had briefly taken up yoga to help her quit vaping. It was one of the less extreme measures she had taken, while the more extreme ones had involved acupuncture and hypnosis. She wished she could say they worked, but each one had been a failed attempt to meditate away her cravings. Only when she had switched one craving for another—aka her vape for snacks and candy—had she been successful.

Hoping her yoga classes weren't all for naught, she breathed in like her instructor had taught her, trying to meditate away the new craving Sal was giving her. It was working about as well as it had in removing her smoking cravings.

When Sal caught a glimpse of her looking at him, she started fanning her face while holding the controller with her other hand. "You're right; it is hot in here. You should turn the air conditioner a bit colder."

Fanning herself faster, she tried to think of a way to get herself off the bed and back downstairs. Fuck the game. If she didn't get out of here, she was going to start licking Sal as if he were a popsicle. One time, she had eaten five popsicles in a single sitting to curb the smoking cravings, so he was in for a real surprise if it came to that.

Sal's fingers started moving on the controller. "Breathing cold air isn't good for you."

"That isn't true," she scoffed, wishing his fingers were playing her instead of the controller, which couldn't appreciate his nimble fingers.

"It's a scientific fact."

She had a scientific fact that she was going to fucking hit him if he didn't turn the air conditioner down or put his shirt back on.

"Why are you trying to bug me?"

"How am *I* bugging *you*?" He said it in a way that he knew exactly what he was doing to bother her.

Sassily, she snapped her fingers in front of his face. "I'm hot. Turn the air down."

"Fine, you win. I'll turn it down." Nonchalantly talking while he took his cell phone from the nightstand, he scrolled through his apps. "Are we going to play, or what?"

Oh, she wanted to play, just not the same game he wanted to. "Yes."

"Well, then pick who you want to be already."

Harassed he wasn't moving from the bed to turn the air down, she chose Yoshi while he, of course, picked Toad.

Sal plunked his cell phone back down on his nightstand. "There. Satisfied?"

"No?" *Am I losing my mind?* she thought, giving him a crazed look. "You haven't even moved from the bed ..."

His steady gaze studied her. "I did it through my thermostat app."

"Of course, you did," Valerie grumbled, looking around at his place. The rich asshole was taking his life in his hands. If she didn't hate jail so bad, she would strangle him.

"You finally ready to play?"

"Mmhmm," she lied, hoping the game would take her mind off licking or killing him.

She and Yoshi were kicking his and Toad's ass in the game ... until Sal shifted on the bed and raised one of his legs, keeping the other one straight. The gray sweatpants tightened at the crotch, showing Sal had a better asset than an apartment she would die for.

"Don't you want to put your shirt back on? The room's cool now."

"Nah, I'm good," he commented lazily.

It honestly didn't even look like he was even trying, and that alone drove her crazier. How could *he* be better than *her*? She wanted to cry. *Hard—Don't say hard!* she screamed at herself.

How could she want to have sex with him? If he hadn't ever helped her with her groceries, he wouldn't be the type of guy who cared if his sexual partner got her cookies off before he got his.

When she lost the game, a string of curses escaped her lips. To be fair, it was hard to concentrate with Sal sprawled out next to her. At least, that was what she told herself.

"This game doesn't count. I'm just getting warmed up." The fact that Sal was, too, didn't matter to her.

When he restarted the game with a smug fucking grin that she wanted to wipe right off his face, she untangled her legs and scooted closer to him until she was practically on his lap. Thinking, *Two can play this game*, she tried to even the playing field ... right up until he shifted again, moving his leg to give her more room, causing Valerie to fumble the controller from trying to get more eye candy.

Yoshi swerved into a guardrail, leaving devastation behind.

"Valerie ..."

Him calling her name had her reluctantly dragging her gaze away from his crotch. She lifted her hot gaze to his, noticing for the first time that his eyes were, in fact, not black like she had thought. They held a deep shade of blue in them, reminding her of the blueish-black shade she liked to dye her hair in. "Yeah ...?"

"You lost."

"I-I did?" She bit her lip hard then lied, "It's your fault. You hit me with a shell. You wanna play again?"

"No." He let his own need finally become apparent. "I want to play something else."

Licking the part of her lip that she had just bitten, she nodded before finally admitting the cold hard truth out loud. "Me, too."

Her admission was all he needed.

Sal lifted then sat her on his hard belly. The fast action took her by surprise, even though she'd had her own plans of plastering herself to him. It wasn't *exactly* how she thought he would make his first move, *but this works*.

Wiggling on him to make herself comfortable, she

thought she had gone to gamer girl heaven. *Oh, this definitely works.*

Suddenly, Sal's hands gripped her hips, stopping her.

"Stop it," he gritted out. "You're going to make me finish before I can get you wet."

Valerie stared down at him unabashedly. "Oh, you are *so* late to that game."

When a satisfied smile played on his lips, her eyes drifted down to them, causing a knot to form low in her belly. Strong hands then slipped down from her waist to the top of her thighs before he spread his fingers out and hooked his thumbs under her panties.

"Kiss me."

He spoke the words with such need that showed he needed this as much as she did, and Valerie didn't have to be told twice. This was a once-in-a-lifetime experience for her, and she wasn't about to let it slip away after waiting for well over twenty years.

Expecting his mouth to be hard, she gave a low moan at how soft it actually was. Barely skimming her mouth across his lips, she grew braver when Sal stayed still. She pressed her lips against his harder and almost swooned when he finally took control. Melding his lips to hers, he parted them, so his tongue could swipe in to tangle with hers.

Jerking her mouth away once she picked up the fresh minty flavor, she straightened to stare him down, which wasn't easy since, technically, he was already down. "You jerk. The least you could have done was to have brought me a mint, too. I'm the one who has Cheeto breath."

"Don't worry; you taste like you," he promised, erasing her fears.

Damn. Who knew Sal could go and say something to make her even hotter?

Figuring she could give him a break with that save, especially since he was doing marvelous things with his thumbs on her clit instead of the controller, she went back to kissing the asshole.

"I like kissing," she admitted against his lips, instantly regretting it when Sal pulled his lips from hers.

Opening his eyes, he gave her a scrutinizing gaze. "Why does it sound like a surprise to you?"

Nervously, she laughed, really wishing she had kept that as an inside thought, especially considering he had stopped his petting altogether, and she had been on the verge of already climaxing.

"Valerie ..."

"Have you never kissed anyone before?" He didn't mean for his voice to come out as harshly as it sounded, but it did. The passion she made him feel, along with the shock of realizing she hadn't been kissed before, was what had caused it. Knowing it was true, he still wanted to hear her say it.

"I haven't." It had taken her a few moments until she was finally brave enough to admit her secret. "The boy I had a crush on in high school told me I was too abrasive for guys to want to kiss me."

"Well, you didn't graduate yesterday, did you?" He couldn't help it. He was still in disbelief.

"No, but I think older guys think I'm abrasive, too." Valerie shrugged before asking, "I mean, I don't think I am. Do you?"

Wisely, Sal kissed her to shut her up. He had been an outcast in school, too. That some guy she liked had told her she was abrasive at a young age and right after puberty made him feel bad for her. I mean, she definitely was a bit abrasive, but the dick didn't have to tell her that.

Using his body, he flipped her onto her back, then rose onto his knees and tugged her panties off before pulling off the shirt he had given her to sleep in. Looking down at her body, he couldn't believe the masterpiece he had just discovered. Underneath the baggy clothes was a sleek body that made him wish he hadn't wasted six months getting the girl next door into his bed. She had a narrow waist with perfect breasts that had him dipping his head to take a peach-colored nipple into his mouth.

Valerie made a sexy sound he had never heard a woman make before. It was filled with need, want, and delight.

The sound filled his chest with pride. He'd been with few women until the last six months. Then he had been with plenty. But each time he had, he'd asked himself if they wanted him for him or because he was one of the only available bachelors left in the Caruso family.

With most of the family members getting married or in long-term relationships, he'd noticed that he was getting hit on more and more with each made men finding love. Sure, it could've been a coincidence, but Sal didn't believe in coincidences. Growing up, he was the one always lurking in the background, and it was no different since joining the Caruso family. All female gazes went mostly to Lucca. He supposed it could have been much worse. If he had been raised as a Luciano, he would have never vied for a female's attention between his brothers Dominic, Angel, and Matthais.

After finally gaining women's affection, that was when he had bought a home. He guessed a part of him was somewhat embarrassed to sleep with a woman in his apartment at the Casino Hotel due to his nosy familial neighbors, not wanting to hear the jokes that he was able to get laid only when the others were taken. Sure, he blamed his lack of sex on being able to see a woman's Internet history, *which was true*, but there had been some women whom he would have gotten with yet knew deep down they were only interested in other made men.

However, with Valerie, he didn't have to think about that.

She was running her hands down his back as if she liked the feel of his skin under her hands. Sal cupped her bottom so he could arch her to his aching cock.

"I like this a lot," she moaned.

"It gets better," he promised, placing a kiss on her throat. "A lot better."

Gliding his finger inside of her, he felt her muscles clamp down. All at once. Sal had to stop sucking on her nipple to rest his forehead on her chest. He didn't have to ask if she was virgin; he felt how tight she was and how she had jumped when his finger entered her.

He didn't have to question why Valerie was untouched. He had played the game she had created, enthralled with the imagination of who had created the world in which bubble gum quicksand entrapped opponents, bubble elevators, and pink guns which shot bubblegum nets. The game was a cross between a Rambo-style retribution and a bubblegum Barbie playland, with various Barbies and Kens playing Rambo. Hours and hours had to have been spent on the game, and from her avatars ... she had a particular type of man she was drawn to. Those were hard to find in real life, which would have led her to disappointment in men in general.

Getting out of his restricting sweatpants, he slid

between her thighs, sliding his cock in position where he could enter her. The need he felt for her practically sent him in shakes as they raced through his body.

Unable to prolong her first-time experience any longer, he bent her legs in the position he wanted so he would be able to thrust deeply inside of her. Ever so slowly, he inched forward.

"Sal ..."

Unexpectedly hearing fear in her voice made him stop.

"You want me to stop?" he heavily breathed. It would kill him to do so, but he would.

"No." The need in her voice matched his. "But you might want to."

He frowned. Sal wouldn't put it past her to have put a trap in her pussy to cut any cock that dared to enter her without her permission. "Why?"

"You're about to enter no man's land," she revealed honestly. "I don't know if you could tell, but I didn't want it to come as a big surprise."

He smiled. It was hard to keep his chuckle in. Of course, he knew. Hell, he had figured as much based on the clothes she wore, and she had pretty much confirmed it when she told him she had never been kissed. Him feeling how tight she was had only solidified his theory.

"I wouldn't have been surprised."

Valerie's blue eyes, that matched the blue in his, almost brimmed with tears. "Are you disappointed?"

"Are you kidding? I ..." He broke off, not wanting her to know he had played her game and already felt at a disadvantage to her avatars. Whether she knew it or not, she was attracted to tall men who were broodingly handsome and built as if they could take on Batman with one hand tied behind their backs. That wasn't him. He had a gun that could get the job done without breaking a sweat. He didn't like to sweat, always thankful for his genes naturally being lean and strong.

"I'm not disappointed," he said thickly before placing a tender kiss on her lips.

When she kissed him back, he started moving again. Pacing his strokes, he thrust in and out of her, gradually increasing the depth of his cock. He only knew he had broken through her hymen when he felt Valerie trying to wiggle away from him. Holding her still, he slowed his pace, letting her adjust to his size until he felt her bucking against him.

God, she feels so fucking good.

Sliding his hand between their bodies, he found her clit, speeding up his thrusts all while stimulating her. Taking Valerie's moans as badges of honor, for some crazy reason, it goaded him on. In turn, he only wanted her to feel the same way, so he put extra care into his motions to do so, wanting her to know just how good sex could feel for her first experience.

A girl like Valerie, who always sought comfort, could easily get burned and swear off sex altogether. As terrible as it sounded, it selfishly made him happy that her first experience, which was always the most memorable, would be owned by him.

Still working her bud, he moved from her mouth to one of her breasts to capture a precious peach nipple. When it came to a peak, his thrusts went deeper than ever as her gasps came faster, alerting Sal that she was about to come. Rising up over her and onto his hands, he powered into her as nails bit into his back.

Her orgasmic cries filled the room while Valerie spiraled out of control, giving him the okay for his owe release. Sal had to hold back his yells of satisfaction, from grinding himself into her until his arms gave out from under him. Falling onto her, he was rewarded with a climax that not only had the bed shaking but his whole world. Six months of pent-up aggression toward one another had finally played out between them, and it took what energy Sal had left to move to the side to give her breathing room.

Exhausted from barely getting any sleep the last two nights, he began dozing off, his arm wrapped snuggly around Valerie's waist. He was sinking into a deep sleep when he felt her move to drape her naked self over his chest.

"Sal?" she whispered.

Barely awake, he lifted one eyelid. "Yeah?"

"Um, how long do we have to wait before we can do it again?"

Does she ever fuckin' sleep?

He managed to wave a hand over his more than satisfied dick. "Depends on what you do to get a rise out of that."

With the lack of response, he closed his eye again, thinking he finally did the impossible of rendering Valerie speechless. Until ...

"Sal?"

"Hmm ..." he mumbled, feeling her light fingertip teasingly circle over his chest.

"Did you know I love popsicles?"

MAKING ME SUICIDAL

"Wake up."

The feeling of something being thrown down on her, along with his voice, had Valerie jolting up in the bed awake.

Dammit! Quickly covering up her exposed breasts, she had forgotten she was bare-ass naked on Sal's bed. When more memories of last night flooded her foggy brain, she wanted to crawl into a hole and die of embarrassment.

Trying to cover up more of her flesh with the sheet, she wasn't sure why it mattered much considering the man fully dressed and staring at her wide-eyed and bushy-tailed this morning had been sucking on her nipples for half the night. Her modesty hadn't just been thrown out the window, it had been tossed out and run over by an armored truck twenty-seven times.

She picked up the items that had been thrown on her with her free hand. "What is this?"

"Clothes," he stated the obvious.

"Yeah, I know that," she grumbled, revealing more of them only for her stomach to feel somehow even sicker than she already did after remembering absolutely everything that had conspired between them last night. She was pretty sure a Nintendo 64 had never led to anything like that before. "But they're girl clothes ..."

"Right. Well, I'm going to make some breakfast." Sal moved right past her statement. "So, hurry up and get dressed."

"Damn, give a girl a chance to wake up before you start ordering her around like a sergeant." She cursed weakly under her breath, so she was sure he could hear as he walked away.

Who the hell does he think he is? And why was he acting so cold to her?

I'm not the one who sent out an invitation to fuck. He was the one who pulled his shirt off before ripping off hers. *Not the other way around, buddy!*

Going into his private bathroom upstairs, she quickly used the bathroom and rinsed off last night's sins before putting on the clothes he had given her.

"Oh no, no, no," she cried when the black jeans clung to her like a second pair of skin. By the time she put on the breast-hugging black top, she was officially certain that, without a doubt, she had fucked a man with a girlfriend and now she was wearing the poor girl's clothes.

If it was at all possible, Valerie would kick her own ass with her bat if she could. "I'm *so* going to hell."

Using his mouthwash that sat on his bathroom counter, she made sure to burn her mouth for as long as she could stand it as punishment for her crimes.

When she left the bathroom and began feeling suffocated from the restricting clothes, she decided to go into Sal's closet real quick, preferring to wear something of his. Big, baggy boy clothes were definitely more her speed. But, of course, she could only see suits hanging up that mostly varied in different navy blue hues. Shockingly, he didn't even have that many, with them only taking up about one-third of the closet. It gave her slight hope that maybe she didn't fuck a man with a girlfriend or perhaps she had recently moved out and now held the title of being an *ex-*girlfriend.

Because he's a cheater!

She was about to start looking through drawers, when she heard her name being yelled out.

"Valerie! Breakfast is ready. Get down here!"

Fuck! Internally cursing, she knew she had run out of time, and this was what she was stuck in until she could get a few things from her house.

She stomped off and down the steps; the smell of pancakes did *slightly* lighten her mood.

"I'm not that good of a cook," he said, placing a plate of pancakes with fruit down in front of her. "But I have learned to cook some things that don't come out of a bag ... or a wrapper."

Her eyes began to turn into slits at his dig, but they quickly grew to normal size when the syrup was set down in front of her. After glazing her pancakes in the sugary good-ness, she took a bite. It was the best thing she'd had eaten in a long while. "Who taught you how to make these?" she asked after swallowing her third huge bite.

Sal, who sat down beside her at the counter, began eating his own helping. "He didn't teach me, really, but I have seen Lucca make them enough times. The secret is a hint of vanill—"

Valerie practically choked to death as she took her fourth bite. "Lucca?" she repeated in disbelief, thinking there was no way she'd heard him correctly. She had to take a sip of the orange juice he had poured out for them to get the lodged piece down.

"Yes." He laughed, understanding her confusion. "He is a surprisingly good cook. Very picky about his food, though ... among other things."

"Lucca? *The* Lucca? The Boogieman? Are you sure we're talking about the same person?" She had to be sure, and then her brain finally went back to the other part of his statement that might be somehow more shocking. "Wait—how have you seen him make pancakes so many times?"

Sal took an awfully long time to swallow his bite. "It's complicated."

"*It's complicated?* Jesus Christ, you gotta give me something here. You can't be making these impossible-to-believe statements and expect me to just walk right past them."

"Sure, I can," Sal said, getting up to place his dishes in the sink. "It's time to go."

"Damn." Watching him rinse the dishes real quick and wave her over to bring her dishes, too, she couldn't help herself. "Did he make you anal about being so tidy and rushing to be on time, too?"

"Valerie, I think that's just called being an adult."

Oh, fuck off, mother—

Fuck, she looks good.

Much preferring her in these clothes, he walked slightly behind her down the hall so he could stare at her ass. Not like he hadn't gotten enough of that view last night, but so what? He was just a man, after all.

The dirty but colorful sneakers that were unfortunately hers that he couldn't get rid of were throwing his fantasy off a bit, but he'd take what he could get … for now. Those, he planned to throw off the top of the building next.

It was no wonder Valerie had been a virgin. She had hidden herself under those outrageously baggy clothes that practically warded off every man in a five-hundred-foot radius. Her face, however, couldn't be dulled by the distraction of her clothes. That was the first thing he had actually noticed about her—the feminine soft beauty of it juxtaposed her usual attire, somehow making her beauty that much more astonishing. But, unfortunately, most men didn't appreciate a good face with freckles. They only appreciated what was *under* the clothes.

Adjusting her shirt because it kept rising up her midriff, she cursed under her breath like she always did. "When are we going back to the house? I need to get a few things if I'm going to stay here for a while. These clothes are killing me."

In that moment, as she pulled her shirt down lower, it only exchanged the view of her exposed stomach to reveal more of her breasts. That was when he contemplated burning her house down and every scrap of clothing she owned.

Never.

WALKING BEHIND SAL INTO WHAT APPEARED TO BE another office, she grew nervous at the unknown. Figuring it was about finding a job here, she couldn't help but feel self-conscious in how she looked. While she dressed like a boy in her usual day-to-day life, she did at least wear business attire to work. Looking professional was the only way a girl could be treated fairly in her male-dominated field. Not to mention she also hated how she hadn't been able to afford to dye her hair lately. Every two weeks on the dot, she freshly box-dyed her hair a blue black, but recently, with every wash, it turned a more denim blue.

In college, she dyed it every color in the rainbow and sometimes all at once, but once she'd gotten her first big-girl job, sadly, the fun colors had to go. The blueish-black shade had at least made her feel more herself, even if it was just a hint of blue in the sun. It would always make her feel special when the blue would shine more. So, while she loved the color her hair was fading into, she knew it would have to go if she got a job here.

Looking down at herself quickly, Valerie would have at least preferred wearing her clothes from yesterday—she didn't care if they had already been worn—but she could only spot her shoes before they'd left his place, having not seen her other clothes ... or her bat, now that she thought about it.

When they were greeted by a beautiful woman with baby-pink hair, she instantly relaxed, feeling right at home. *Oh, thank God, someone normal!*

The perks of being in the mafia were really starting to rack up at this point.

"Hi, I'm Katarina," she introduced herself with a smile. "But you can call me Kat."

"You're Sal's sister?" She was taken aback by another surprise; never would she have guessed that the two were related. Kat looked so ... *cool*, while Sal had such a stick up his ass.

"Yes." She laughed, figuring she couldn't see the family resemblance. "My brother has told me a lot about you, Valerie. So, it's nice to put a face to the name."

Oh, I'm sure he did. Knowing Sal, he probably had a lot to say about her. She figured she should be embarrassed, but his sister wasn't at all making her feel like she should. In fact, she seemed to love that Valerie was a pain in his ass. "It's nice to meet you, too."

"I'm glad my clothes worked out for you," Kat said, eyeing her approvingly.

"Oh!" Valerie took a breath of relief to at least not be meeting Sal's sister in his girlfriend's clothes. It made her feel like she was slightly *less* of a home wrecker, which was good. "They're your clothes. I see it now," she said, pointing back and forth at their attire. Kat, too, was wearing tight jeans and a top. Valerie only wished Sal would have bothered taking a cool leather jacket out of her closet, too. "I love your jacket."

"Thanks. I offered Sal to give you—"

Sal loudly coughed, interrupting her words and butting into the end of her sentence. "So, do you have anything Valerie could do around here? The court won't let her use a computer or anything, but I'm hoping you could find something for her."

Again, Valerie should maybe feel embarrassed that another complete stranger knew of her criminal situation. But at this point, and especially after she stood there while Sal continued to pretend like nothing had happened last night between them, her life was a joke.

"Yes, I've actually been needing an assistant. I got a bit behind on some paperwork."

"That's perfect." With his phone beeping, Sal became distracted easily. "I'll be by in a few hours to check on you two. Kat, be sure to keep an eye on this one, and Valerie ..."

She tried not to roll her eyes at that comment and scolding tone.

"I'm trusting you won't give my sister any trouble?"

I'll fucking give you some trouble, bitc—

"Yeah, yeah, I think we got it from here," Kat shooed her brother out of her office, sensing the tension. It was like she knew Valerie and her imp so well already.

Waving her hand, she gave Sal a big, satisfying smile as the door slammed right in his face.

Already, Valerie could tell she and Kat were about to become fast friends. They looked opposite but weirdly the same. Different but similar. Yin and yang.

"Sorry about him," Kat apologized on his behalf. "I think he's just been a bit stressed lately. Just work, I'm sure."

Interesting ... Or a breakup perhaps?

Kat got right to it, showing Valerie how to sort through some paperwork that had piled up and in which files in the cabinet she should place them.

After giving her the rundown on her detailed, color-coded filing system, Kat finally asked, "Any questions?"

"Yes, I do have one ..." It was a lot to take in, but Valerie only had one question in mind. "Does Sal have girlfriend?"

ONLY AN HOUR HAD PASSED BEFORE A TEXT CAME through on his phone. Seeing it was his sister messaging him, he instinctively knew exactly what it was going to be about.

"Fuck."

After reading the words, *Get here now*, he left his security office to head to Kat's. By the time he got there, she was outside the door, waiting for him.

"Don't worry; she's in there," Kat immediately spoke, sensing he thought she had run off.

"Why the hell have you left her alone?" Sal harped; they both knew she was a flight risk. The only reason he trusted his sister to watch her was because, unlike him, Katarina had grown up as a Luciano with his other brothers, Dominic, Angel, Matthais, and Cassius. She not only kept all of them in line from time to time, but hell, she kept her poor husband, Drago, practically whipp—

"What do you think she's going to do? Jump out the window and fall one hundred fifty feet to her death?"

Her deadpan face had Sal taken aback, knowing his sister had a point there.

"She's the one making *me* suicidal, not her."

Sal's hand went to massage his temples. He was already getting a headache from his lack of sleep. He didn't need this. "Christ. What did she do? I'm sure she had a hard time following direction—"

"Oh no." Kat stopped him right there. "She can follow directions just fine and did everything I asked immediately. I was behind filing two weeks' worth of paperwork, and she filed them perfectly within thirty minutes."

Sal wasn't exactly seeing the problem, then. "Okay ...?"

"She's spent the last thirty minutes with her feet up, asking me things like, *Does Sal have a girlfriend? How can I join the mafia?* Or, *do you have any Twizzlers?*"

"Goddammit," Sal huffed, going back to rubbing his temples. "Well, maybe you can find something else for her to do—"

"Oh, no, no, no." Kat waved her hands violently against that idea. "Listen, love her to death, and I can't wait to hang out with her *outside* of this office, but ... she can't work here."

Sal desperately tried to take a deep and calming breath but gave up. "Okay, I understand."

"Sorry, Sal." She looked at him pityingly but not too

pityingly that she would change her mind. "I just have way too much work to do, and she's *a bit* distracting."

Knowing his sister was trying to be nice by saying *a bit*, he knew it was more like *a lot a bit*. "Tell me about it," he mumbled under his breath before shoving open the door to find Valerie shooting staples out of a stapler. "Let's go."

Putting down the joke of a loaded weapon, Valerie hurried out of the office. "Something wrong—Bye, Kat! See ya later!" she tossed over her shoulder to the waving woman when Sal grabbed her hand and dragged her along down the hallway.

You could say that. YOU.

But Sal didn't say those words out loud. Too afraid he'd lose his temper with any of her responses that always held a bit of sarcasm. Trying to cool himself, he knew this wasn't like him. He was the cool, calm, collected, and responsible one in the family, and Valerie was driving him insane right along with her.

"Jesus, Sal." She snatched her hand out of his grasp and put her foot down. "Where the hell are we going?"

Truthfully, he knew he wanted to take her right back to his place here at the Casino Hotel and fuck her brains out again, but that fact scared him.

Absolutely terrified him.

Never in his life had he ever fucked a woman twice.

Sure, he had stopped looking women up on the web when he wanted to sleep with them; otherwise, he'd still be a virgin. But he always broke and did so after the first encounter. Sal knew his downfalls, and becoming easily attached was one. He had his childhood to thank for that.

But falling fast and hard for a woman who had returned a dog to a shelter or still cyberstalked her ex wasn't the one.

It didn't matter how small the offense was, or if she Googled *Do dogs have souls?*

Everything always gave him a reason to never sleep with them again.

He still remembered looking her up before he bought the house next door to her and found practically nothing but basic information. Hell, he hated to admit it, but it was why he'd decided to sign on the dotted line.

So, imagine his surprise that the woman with no social media or problematic Internet history was the reason he regretted ever buying it.

"Sal ..." She snapped her fingers in front of his face to bring him back to reality. *"Where. Are. We. Going?"*

He hit the elevator button that lit up with the down arrow. There was no way in hell she could work in the main casino, but she could somewhere else. "Underground."

NOT IN KANSAS CITY ANYMORE

The door being guarded by the big bald man told her they were not in Kansas City anymore. Wherever this place was, it was a well-kept secret.

She found it strange when the bodyguard didn't open the door immediately. It wasn't until Sal gave him a threatening glance that he gave in.

Well, that wasn't strange at all, she thought when he finally gave in and moved to the side, opening the door for them. Nothing could have prepared her for what she walked into as a packed casino that was different than the one that sat above it was revealed.

Valerie was really beginning to feel like a broken record at this point. "Sal, where the hell are we?"

"An illegal underground casino." The way he said it was like it was no big deal.

Taking a look around at all the hot women in the tiny, scantily-clad outfits serving men drinks, or taking their chips from behind the tables, she finally just shrugged like it was, in fact, no big deal after all. "Well, all righty, then."

Sal looked over at her, suspiciously surprised. "This isn't a problem for you?"

She raised a brow. "Everyone in here eighteen or older?"

He nodded. "Yep."

"And do they all get paid well?" she asked, raising the other one.

"Very well."

"Then I see no issue." She then went on to something much more important as she pointed to a blonde in a hot-pink lace bra and panties with matching garters. "Now, I don't have to wear anything like that, do I?"

"HELL NO!"

The words flung out of his mouth like an upchuck. The passion he felt behind those words surprised even him, let alone Valerie. He couldn't help it. All he imagined was her in one of the three-piece lingerie sets the girls wore, and it sent him into orbit with the thought of one of the regulars down here getting a look at her ass.

Sal wiped the bead of sweat that coated his brow. *Fucking hell, am I sexually frustrated?*

Holy fuck, he was. This was only the beginning of having to deal with Valerie, and he was already about to kill himself.

Goddamn, his sister was right. She did have an effect of making you suicidal.

"Are you okay?" Valerie asked, noticing the action.

"I'm fine," he snapped at her, desperately wishing to put space between them. It didn't help he was in his favorite place in the world and felt some sudden withdrawals coming on.

"Geez, excuse me for being concerned for your fucking well-being. I thought after last night's festivities, I could ask things like that." Sick of his shitty attitude and treatment all day, she had reached a breaking point. "By the way, you're the one who fucked me last night, so I'm not sure why you're taking it out on me!"

"Please, your eyes were practically begging me for it," he reminded her.

"Yeah, right." Valerie snorted. "The only one begging for it was you, Mr. It's Hot in He—Ow!"

She rubbed her arm that he bumped to shut her up when a big man in a suit came up to them. His looks were a bit deceiving the closer he got, as there was a bit of youngness to his face that told her he wasn't as old as he appeared to be ... but he sure was hot.

"Well, well, well ..." The man approached them with a killer smile. "Now, you know you're not supposed to be down here, Sal—"

Valerie's eyes grew wider as she continued listening, hanging on to his every word.

"The last time you fucking snuck down here almost cost me a year's worth of my salary 'cause Lucca made me pay for not noticing you had gotten down here—"

"Yeah, whatever, Amo." Sal stopped him. "I'm not down here for that."

"I see." Amo's eyes slid over to her before looking her up and down from head to toe appreciatively. "New recruit?"

No wonder Lucca hates his fuckin' guts.

Suddenly, Sal perfectly understood Lucca's hatred for the man in front of him. He thought his best friend was a bit harsh to his younger brother Nero's friend. It wasn't like it was Amo's fault he fell in love with the same girl Lucca had.

But seeing his eyes get an eyeful of Valerie, he already knew his late-night activities tonight would be searching up porn with a featured woman that most resembled Valerie.

I oughta take Valerie's bat and shove it right up his as—

Rubbing his hands together, Amo was already playing dress up in his mind. "She'll fit right in down here. We've been looking for a girl with a different look."

Yup, he was going to do it. He was going to shove that bat right up his ass and video tape the whole thing. Sal couldn't possibly move up any more in the family business, but he bet he somehow could if he did it and gave the tape to Lucca for his viewing pleasure.

"Been a bit boring lately down here, don't you think, Sal?"

At Amo's comment, Valerie took a better look at the girls walking around in their underwear. Remembering one, then another, then another …

It was practically Sal's graveyard of women he had taken back to his house and fucked, and now he was here, adding his latest lay to his collection.

The man didn't have a fucking girlfriend; he had a slew of women, ripe for the picking, an elevator ride away.

Valerie didn't know whether to feel ashamed, mad, or

honestly a little bit proud that she was among some of the fine women down here.

But, somehow, despite her frustration toward Sal at the moment, there was a small silver lining in all of this.

I'm no longer a home wrecker.

THE LAUGHING FIT THAT ESCAPED VALERIE'S LIPS HAD both men staring at her in concern.

What in the hell is so funny?

"So, you don't have a girlfriend!" she burst out in what seemed like relief.

"Who? Sal?" Amo asked, laughing himself into his own fit. He understood exactly what was so funny. "Hell no! He can barely let himself get laid."

Suddenly, Valerie's laughter subsided.

"You done, Amo?" Sal's voice came out calmer than he'd thought it would. "Or maybe I can tell Lucca how you—"

"What do you need?" Amo quickly asked in fear.

Gaining control of the situation, he was finally able to get to the point. "She needs a job that doesn't involve using a computer, *and* she has to be watched over at all times." When Amo gave him a confused look, he added, "Flight risk," for clarity.

That seemed to clear up any of Amo's confusion as he asked, "Anything in particular?"

"Yeah," Sal began to make himself very clear, "one where she preferably keeps the clothes she's currently wearing *on*."

"Oh, I can definitely work with that." Amo gave her

another appreciative look and held out his elbow for her to take. "Come on, doll. What's your name?"

The smile she gave Amo before she wound her hand around the offered arm sent Sal over the edge. Only the first three letters of her name had come out of her mouth before he snatched her ass right back.

"Val—"

"You know what? Never mind," Sal told Amo before dragging her back out through the Underground.

"What the—Sal!" she snapped and hit at his arm as he pulled her through the Casino Hotel yet again. Out of breath and baseball bat-less, she gave up, letting him take her to another floor.

The room he took her into this time was a darkened space with a million different screens that watched over all the guests in the Casino Hotel, with only one person watching them who hadn't even bothered to peel his eyes away from the screens. Oddly enough, she found it calming. It was kinda like watching over a video game with multiple avatars. She wasn't in the room long when she was led yet again through another door and into someone's office.

Who's the lucky person I'm going to meet now?

Internally, she rolled her eyes, waiting for the made man to show up that she was going to attempt to shadow next.

Rolling in another chair from the screen room, he placed it right by the door he had just shut them into. "Sit here."

Valerie sank to the chair he had pushed her down on, the feeling awfully similar to being put in timeout as a child. With nothing to do, she couldn't help but notice the computer setup of her fucking dreams. Whoever owned it, she definitely wanted to meet now. Hell, she wanted to have sex with the man on the desk.

So, imagine her surprise when Sal sat down behind it.

"This is *your* office?"

Sal reached into the front pocket of his suit and put on his glasses before he looked at the multiple screens.

So, he does wear glasses! Blue light glasses.

When he began typing on his keyboard, the sound of it was so satisfying she wanted to run her fingertips across him —er, *the keyboard.*

"Mmhmm," he mumbled, already drifting into a different world as he looked at the screens.

"Oh." Biting her lip, Valerie suddenly stopped slumping and sat up in the computer chair straighter. She couldn't believe he never struck her as a computer guy before, as he fit in so well behind it. At least she felt a little better now after getting her ass beat in Mario Kart. "I see. And *what* exactly is your job title?" Her voice had turned sweet as butter, but she was in for yet another surprise.

"Head of security."

Feeling a bit warm inside, all she could manage to fluster out was, "T-That's nice." God, he was just so hot behind a computer screen.

"So ..." She managed to pull herself together. "Is that for just the Casino Hotel or the family ...?"

"It's kind of a package deal," he said, distracted by his work as he continued to type away. Only when she had become silent for too long, as it was unlike her, did he finally look at her to notice she was dying to ask him another question. "You need something?"

In that moment, Valerie knew exactly what she wanted. "Wanna fuck?"

CODE PINK

The knock on the door had Valerie sitting up naked in bed. *Oh, shit.*

After the two had gone from fucking on the desk in his office to fucking on the bed in his penthouse, she had completely forgotten something.

This time, the words actually left her mouth. "Oh, shit!"

"Don't worry about it. It's fine. Whoever it is can come back late—"

"No!" she cried, jumping out of bed to put her clothes on. "I forgot I invited your sister over for a game night."

Sal jumped out of bed within a second to start getting dressed himself. "Now, why the hell did you do that?"

"Because she has a PlayStation, duh!" She added the last flourishing word like it was obvious.

Sal rolled his eyes heavenward. "Of course."

While running down the steps, she smoothed down her tousled hair before opening the door, hoping the sins she had just committed with her brother wouldn't be obvious to Kat.

"Hey, Valerie ..." Kat's smile slightly fell upon taking in

her appearance. "You still wanted to have a game night, right?"

"Oh yeah, of course. Why wouldn't I?" Her cheeks went ablaze.

"Oh, good. I just wanted to be sure because you don't have a phone, and I tried texting Sal to confirm, but I didn't get a respons—"

"Hey, sis!" Sal came down with awkwardness, making it all the more obvious that they had just done it. "Come on in. Sorry I missed your texts."

"It's not a problem," Kat said, coming inside, but as she passed, she whispered something for only Valerie's ears to hear. "Your shirt is inside out."

"Thanks," she whispered back before desperately trying to laugh it off. "I'll be right back."

She stepped away for a moment to go in the downstairs bathroom to freshen herself up a bit in the mirror and turn her shirt right-side out, thinking at this point, *Just how more embarrassing can my life get?*

When she came out of the bathroom, however, to her surprise, Sal's living room was filled with more girls.

Valerie waved at them a bit nervously, thinking how pretty they all were. She couldn't help but wonder how many of them Sal had slept with. They all smiled warmly at her, and she instinctively knew not a one had, except for her.

"Everyone, this is Valerie," Katarina began the introductions. "Valerie, this is Elle …"

A girl with strawberry-blonde hair waved.

"Lake."

The tall model-like brunette waved next.

"Adalyn."

A short and cute-as-a-button brunette girl waved after her name was announced.

"Gianna."

An obvious Italian woman nodded. She appeared to be the least girly one out of the bunch.

"And Chloe."

This one had given her a tender but somewhat shy smile. The black-haired, porcelain-skinned beauty took her breath away, along with the scars marking the left side of her face. There had been a couple characters in her video game she had kept changing the appearance of. One in particular gave her the most trouble, because she didn't know what was missing from the female character's look, so she had finally given up and settled on a look she wasn't fond of before she'd sent her game off to Game Hookup. If it wasn't for losing her job and needing to eat, she would have never sent it off before some of the characters' looks were fully fleshed out. Now she knew, standing there, looking at the woman named Chloe, that her female character was missing badass scars.

"Hello, everyone." Valerie smiled at them all, somehow feeling welcomed instantly.

Kat then explained the extra faces. "I thought game night would be more fun if I invited all the girls to join. I hope that's okay?"

"Of course, it is," she agreed, noticing the game Kat had brought with her, already thinking of all the KOs she planned to accumulate in Mortal Kombat. "The more, the merrier."

"Well, I'm going to leave you girls to it," Sal announced, heading for the door, visibly ready to leave. "I'll let you all enjoy your little girls' night. I think Gianna can handle it from here."

Understanding why Gianna appeared different, Valerie figured she must be a bodyguard of some sorts, which explained the black slacks and shirt. *Hell yeah.* She was going to have to find a way to add her to her video game, too.

Sal waved goodbye one last time before opening the door, and when he did, the most gorgeous blonde Valerie had ever seen in her life suddenly materialized.

"Oh, hell nah." Sal tried to stop the woman from entering by immediately shutting the door in her face.

With pounding hitting the other side of the door, you could hear the woman's irritated voice. "What the fuck is your deal, Sal?"

But he stood firm. "You can't come in!"

"Don't make me call your older brother to come down here. 'Cause you know Dominic will!"

At her threat, the door let up.

"Now, step aside," she ordered and passed with the click of her pointy high heels.

Seeing the huge rock on the woman's finger killed all hope of Valerie getting to marry her. Never in her life had she been so jealous of a man, knowing instantly that whoever Dominic was, he was one lucky man.

"So, what are we doing tonight, girls?" The perfect blonde asked, smoothing down her baby-pink women's suit that the altercation had messed up. The gold buttons that adorned her suit told Valerie that the unknown woman was the most expensive thing in the room.

"Well, we thought we could play some Mortal Kombat," Kat said, showing her they had company. "Valerie here is big into video games."

"Oh, I'm sorry, Valerie. Where are my manners?" The woman flipped her blonde locks over her shoulders before smiling.

In that moment, Valerie could hear Sal crying in the distance, but she paid him no mind.

"I'm Maria. Maria Caruso."

And I think I'm in love.

GODDAMMIT.

Sal hung his head low in defeat before he shut the door back in place with him still on the same side. There was no way he was going anywhere with these two in the same room. Only God knew what would happen, and he was pretty certain that with *all* the Caruso women in a single room, it could be the start of female world domination.

"Where are you going?" Kat asked him as he headed back upstairs in solitude.

"Unfortunately, nowhere," he spat back.

"But I thought you were leaving?" Valerie blurted out after her eyes left Maria's.

"Changed my mind."

"Fine ..."

"Suit yourself ..."

"All righty." A different response came out of each girl's mouth, all while laughing as he did the walk of shame back upstairs.

He used to make fun of the guys for being whipped by their women, but it was no wonder they were. He could practically feel Valerie's bat being slung already.

After the performance upstairs and in his office, Sal was certain he'd do crazy things to have sex with Valerie again. She had officially smashed his record of times he'd had sex with the same woman, and he was already planning for another repeat performance.

There certainly were perks to fucking a girl who was a loose cannon, but the last thing he needed was for Crazy Valerie to meet Psycho Maria. Maria had only become more psychotic, as well, since becoming a mother to her daughter, Angelica.

Pulling his phone out of his pocket, he thought the world as they knew it depended on him, so he started a mass text ...

COME GET YOUR WOMEN!!!

"I'll do it," Valerie volunteered herself to hook the PlayStation up. She never minded and always enjoyed doing it.

She moved behind the TV, and as she started hooking the game system up, she quickly noticed something. The TV *had* been wired for the Nintendo 64 after all.

I knew it! At feeling vindicated that Sal was the one who had wanted to fuck her first, her smug smile suddenly turned sweet. It was kind of cute that he'd done that, even if it was just to get in her pants. It especially didn't bother her considering she was happy to no longer be an un-kissed virgin.

Smiling to herself, she finished. "All done."

"What's that smile for?" Maria was the only one brave enough to ask.

She wiped the grin off her face with cheeks burning red. "Nothing."

"That's definitely not nothing." Adalyn winked at her, agreeing with Maria.

"Guys, leave her alone." She thought Kat was sparing her, but that quickly changed. "I think she might have a crush."

With a collective gasp from her newfound friends, they all chided in with different things.

"A crush!"

"*Ooo.*"

"On whom?"

"*That,* I won't tell." Kat locked her mouth and threw away the key.

"I do not," Valerie refuted loudly but quickly turned her voice as low as humanely possible, "have a crush!"

"Oh my God, you so do," Maria realized, putting two and two together before almost gagging to death. "On Sal!"

"I can fucking hear you!" Sal screamed over the banister at hearing Maria's incessant gagging noises. He was about to throw up all over her if she didn't knock it off.

"Well, no one told you to listen!" Maria screamed up at him.

"Yeah," Kat butted in. "It's girls' night; you're not supposed to be here to listen to girl talk, anyway."

If he didn't get them out of here, he was never going to get laid again. All he needed was for Maria to tell Valerie something stupid he did growing up to give her the ick.

Sal picked up the phone and sent another text in hopeless desperation, knowing his dick depended on it.

CODE PINK!

Valerie stood, listening to them bicker, swearing that the way Maria talked with Sal was that of a sister. She figured it was just because she was married to his brother; that could be the only explanation as to why.

She was about to open her mouth but didn't dare knowing Sal could overhear.

"Hang on." Gianna threw on some music, understanding her predicament. All of them were now unconcerned with the reason they had come over in the first place —to play video games. They wanted in on the latest gossip instead.

As they huddled together in a girl puddle like they were fifteen at a sleepover, Valerie felt comfortable enough to talk in a low tone, knowing that he couldn't hear a thing over the obnoxiously loud music.

"Okay, fine!" she muttered loudly, admitting defeat. "I *might* have a crush on Sal."

"I knew it!" Maria hissed triumphantly. "But also ... *ew*."

"Why *ew*? Why *ew*?" Valerie countered, afraid that she was missing something about him and maybe shouldn't have ever slept with him in the first place ... As if the basement full of women wasn't enough; somehow, she'd let herself walk by that massive red flag.

"Oh, please," Gianna shushed Maria. "It's only gross to her because she sees him as a brother."

Maria nodded. "True."

Taking the biggest sigh of relief, she instantly relaxed. "Oh, good."

"Sal's totally hot," Gianna continued expressing her approval. "These girls won't agree 'cause they all have their· own men, but take it from me: you might have got the best of the bunch."

"Hey!"

"Easy, now!"

"Yeah, watch it!" the other girls hissed in offense,

reminding Gianna to tread lightly when talking about their significant others.

"Listen," Kat chimed in to give her own thoughts, "as someone who grew up a Luciano but married one of the Carusos, along with the fact that he's my brother, so I have free rein to tell the truth ... I can tell you that Gianna's right. Sal's a good person, and he *really* isn't like the rest."

"As much as I hate to admit it." Maria almost threw up again but clearly wanted to clarify her feelings. "She's right. And this is coming from someone who grew up with the Carusos but married a Luciano ... The Caruso men are, well ... entitled—"

"Mmhmm," the girls agreed in unison.

Maria threw up another manicured finger to go with the one she already had up. "Arrogant ..."

"Yep!" they said, chiming in again.

Another finger. "Asses."

"So true," all the girls agreed, backing her up one last time.

Valerie thought back over those words.

Entitled, arrogant, ass ...

"And Sal *isn't* one?" 'Cause, to her, it sounded just like him.

"Oh, honey"—Maria patted her hand—"you must not have met the others yet."

"I've met Lucca and Amo."

The girls went eerily quiet.

Kat cleared her throat, daring to ask, "And what did you think?"

"Scary and hot," Valerie revealed before explaining her answer. "Lucca, *scary*. Amo, *hot*."

All the girls busted out in laughter, except for one. Chloe.

"Lucca's not scary," the scarred woman said a bit defensively.

"Of course, he's not to you," Gianna told her before getting her laughter under control. "Amo is hot, though; I have to agree. But you don't think he was an ass?"

"Oh yeah, totally," Valerie agreed. "But Sal's a bigger one, and for some reason, he scared Amo. Wait—" Her brain finally picked up on what had been said earlier in the conversation. "How is Sal a Caruso but also related to your husband, who's a Luciano?" Her brain even hurt trying to say it, let alone begin to understand it.

The two mob families of KC were notorious for their feud, up until recently, when she'd heard whispers of a possible truce.

All the girls looked at her pityingly in that moment.

"He hasn't told you anything yet, has he?" Maria realized.

Shaking her head, she wished Sal had revealed anything at all to her about himself. Hell, if it wasn't for her neighbor, she wouldn't have even known his name.

Maria just patted her hand again. "Honey, we need to talk."

SAL LISTENED TO THE SONG "MILKSHAKE" BLARING over his stereo system while he listened to the girls whispering and laughing between the oooing and ahhing. If he heard *"my milkshakes bring all the boys to the yard"* one more fuckin' time, he was going to lose it. It didn't help he couldn't hear what they were saying, meaning he already assumed the worst and that Valerie would hear anything and everything to make her never want to sleep with him again.

In a final desperate attempt, he added one more person to the mass group chat before texting ...

HOT GIRLS AT MY PLACE

Christ.

He just had to pray awakening the playboy wouldn't bite him in the ass.

WHILE THE GIRLS FINALLY STARTED UP THE PlayStation, both her and Maria spoke in their own hushed conversation in the kitchen.

"So, is Sal a *Caruso* or *Luciano?* I'm so confused," she asked, trying to get clarification.

"A Caruso," Maria revealed like it was just that easy to understand. However, it clearly wasn't as she continued, "But, technically, he should be a Luciano by blood, considering his father and siblings are all Lucianos."

"Okay ..." That only made Valerie even more confused, and it made her question Maria's intelligence. "And how does that happen?"

Sadness crossed Maria's beautiful features until she waved her hand toward the kitchen stool. "You'll want to take a seat."

A BATTLE OF BLOODY GUTS AND GLORY

Wanting to cry at Sal's past left Valerie heartbroken for him. Even her own broken past seemed to pale in comparison to his. She couldn't imagine growing up homeless, only to find out a father didn't want you but accepted his other legitimate children in his life, not to mention his mother's tragic death, along with being taken in by his father's enemy.

"I only told you all this 'cause I've looked at Sal as a brother since we grew up together."

It made sense, the bickering not only between Sal and Maria, but with Lucca as well. They had all lived under the same roof officially since Sal was thirteen years old.

"I know he should have been the one to tell you, but I can tell you like him, and that he must like you *on account of how badly he didn't want me to meet you.*" She added that bit still annoyed but continued on, getting serious again. "I just think you should know what you're dealing with because out of all the years I've spent with him, he still doesn't like to talk about it."

"Are you serious?" Valerie almost couldn't believe it. At

that rate, she'd be old and dead before he'd tell her anything. "Not to anyone?"

"I think he talks about it with my brother, but Lucca wouldn't dare tell me anything that Sal told him in confidence."

Wishing it had been Sal to be the one to tell her, she was still grateful Maria had. Everything about Sal had clicked into place. To say she had misjudged him was the understatement of the fucking century. Valerie officially not only felt like the biggest idiot in the world, but the biggest bitch as well. She couldn't believe some of the thoughts and preconceived notions she'd had about him.

Sal hadn't grown up rich with a stick up his ass; he had grown up with nothing and treasured the items he had, along with his privacy. Regretting certain things she had said and done to him, she desperately wished she could take them all back. But, in life, there were no do-overs. She would have to live with it forever. It was truly no wonder why Sal hated her at first. She was just thankful for the fact that their relationship had blossomed into whatever the hell it was at the moment.

Feeling her heart skip a beat for the first time in her life, she found herself wanting a relationship, hoping that what was between her and Sal wouldn't be fleeting and that when all her legal troubles were over, that maybe, just maybe, they could gain more out of each other than smart-witted comebacks and sex.

"Thank you for telling me, Maria," she whispered. "I had no idea Sal and Lucca were even that close."

"Oh yes, they are closer to brothers than probably Lucca's blood brothers. There's a bit of an age difference between them, so that's mostly why," Maria explained before laughing. "If I had been born a boy, I probably would have given Sal a run for his money as his favorite brother."

"That reminds me ..." Valerie pivoted the subject with hope in her eyes. "How exactly does a woman go about joining the mafia?"

A KNOCK ON THE DOOR HAD SAL JUMPING TO HIS FEET and almost killing himself to get down the steps.

Thank Go—Fuck! It was probably too late. Maria and Valerie were already talking in the kitchen for God knew how long.

"Who is it?" Maria asked, seeing him whizz by.

"Backup," was his response, flinging open the door to see who it was. Of course, *he* had gotten here first.

Figures.

WATCHING LUCCA CARUSO WALK INTO THE ROOM FELT eerily strange. No longer in his deadly all-black suit, he wore a sweatshirt and dark jeans. It looked so informal on him but also so right. Now she could start to understand why the other girls found him attractive. He was no longer dressed as the Boogieman but himself, so his looks turned less sinister and more ruggedly handsome.

"Time to go, Chloe." With a commanding voice, he waved for her to move.

Noticing the wedding band on his ring finger for the first time, Valerie's mouth fell right down to the floor. *He's married to* her!

Her mind was blown for the millionth time today.

Never in all her life of playing video games could she have predicted that plot twist coming. How in the world a sweet and shy, scarred woman had ended up with the Boogieman would defy her imagination for the rest of her existence.

It was obvious Chloe didn't want to go. "But Maria's babysitter is watching the twins for the night, with Angelica. Can't we stay for a bit longer?"

Jesus! They procreated?

Lucca shook his head more defiantly. "We're leaving—now."

The poor woman's hair covered her face as she set the controller down in sadness, clearly having a good time. While all the girls' faces were upset she was leaving, not one dared to question it, not even Maria.

Valerie's heart sank for her, but before she could let the woman leave, she just couldn't help herself and had to ask, "Chloe"—she stepped before the couple, who were complete opposites in every way, keeping them from leaving just yet—"would you mind giving me a picture of yourself?"

"W-Why?" she asked nervously, making Valerie hate herself for asking it that way before explaining. Even the way Lucca was staring at her, while in a curious way, was making her uncomfortable, as it was obvious his protective instincts were coming out. Hell, the whole room had fallen silent, as everyone had heard her and was too curious as to what kind of question that was.

She had seen this whole interaction go differently in her head. Sometimes, she really hated her big mouth but just had to go with it at this point.

"Well, I've been working on a video game, and if you don't mind, I'd love to model one of my female characters after you?"

"Oh ... wow," Chloe said. Taken aback, it took her a

moment before she brushed the hair behind her ears, proudly displaying her scars. "Sure."

With Lucca relaxing his grip on his wife's hand, he let her go. "We can stay a bit longer."

"Hell yeah!" Kat cried gleefully, holding the controller back out for her. "We get another rematch."

When Chloe returned to the game with a smile, Lucca gave Valerie an approving look. "Sal ..."

GETTING A BIT CHOKED UP AT THAT KIND INTERACTION, he bit down the emotion welling in his throat. The action had made not only Sal grow fond of her in an instant, but Lucca Caruso himself. And Valerie didn't have a clue what she had just accomplished.

"Yeah?" he asked, already dreading what might come next.

"You find her a job yet?"

"Not exactly." He ran his fingers through his hair, knowing his boss wasn't going to be happy. "It's been a bit *difficult* to place her. She—"

"Try harder, then," Lucca cut him off.

Sal could only nod his head, accepting the order. *Christ,* for better or for worse, he was stuck with Valerie's antics now. It shocked him to find that he was surprisingly happy about it, too. Once you gained Lucca's favor, especially through the way of his wife, he did everything in his power to make sure you were cared for. If Kent Bryant didn't find a way to get her charges dropped, *and soon,* the lawyer was going to have hell to pay.

"Give her whatever job she wants," Lucca said before ending the conversation to go sit beside his wife.

Instinctively knowing Valerie's big mouth was about to ruin the moment, he reached out to grab her hand and stop her from going after Lucca.

"Don't press your luck," he told Valerie quietly, hoping she'd take the hint.

"*Fine*," she finally grumbled, "I won't ask him if I can join the family."

Only when she made him a promise that she wouldn't did Sal let her go, somewhat satisfied.

"I'd be staking my claim if I were you ..." a taunting female voice from behind him said, as if she knew he had just called in the cavalry. "Before the ones who aren't married get here."

Dammit. He hated when Maria made perfect sense.

He moved to a closet and took out the clothes he had hidden, along with her bat, in case Valerie became inclined to use it on any of the guests about to walk in. She did have the boss' permission, after all.

"Why are you giving me these now?" she asked after he handed them to her.

"Because I need you to change—"

Suddenly, her usual attire was perfect for her. Hell, he loved it. The more hideous and baggy the clothes she wore, the better as far as he was concerned. If it could ward off any of the men who were about to walk through the door, it would save him from a fight.

"*Now*." He tried his best to sound as commanding as Lucca had with his woman, because Sal's mind had been made up within an instant.

Valerie Monroe was his.

WHEN MORE MEN CAME BARRELING THROUGH, Valerie's mouth dropped farther and farther open. The Caruso-Luciano gene pool was unmatched.

Nero Caruso, who was Elle's boyfriend, was a mix of his siblings Maria and Lucca, if that gave you an idea on how good-looking he was. Which brought her to the next guest being Dominic Luciano, who was the only one capable of rivaling Lucca's presence. *Badass motherfucker* was what came to her mind upon seeing him show up in a leather coat with fur around the collar.

His brother, Angel Luciano, who was dating Adalyn, was covered head to toe in tattoos. She desperately needed to ask him to model for a character in her game as well.

Then, when a piercing blue-eyed blond walked in, she could see the hint of redness in his eyes. Like he had been crying. His name was Vincent, and he was quiet as he took a seat beside Lake. Valerie wondered what it was he had been upset about.

By the time Amo tried barreling through, Sal had worked himself up into a jealous fit that she thought was kind of cute. Valerie didn't even think he realized he was the jealous type yet. She knew why he had given her her clothes back, but she didn't mind, happy to feel like herself again.

"What the hell are you doing here?" Sal asked him bluntly.

Amo was immediately offended. "Damn, what's *that* supposed to mean?"

"Meaning I didn't invite you. You don't have a girlfriend or wife here. Who the hell told you, anyway?"

Valerie was worried all hell was about to break loose when Amo stood defiantly. "I'm not at liberty to say ..."

Sal turned to give dirty looks to all the men in the room, wondering who the hell had invited him, but not a one dared to tell the truth.

Amo wasn't the playboy Sal had called in as a last-ditch effort to bribe the men into breaking up girls' night. That one had yet to show and was much more dangerous for Valerie to meet. If he was lucky, he could get everyone to leave before that person showed up.

"Well, party's ove—"

"But I haven't gotten to play Mortal Kombat yet." Amo stopped him from closing the door in his face when no one else took Sal seriously that the party was, in fact, over.

Sal was about to slam his fingers in the door when Valerie stepped in, giving Sal a dirty look. "Come on inside, Amo; you can verse me."

Those words only made him want to kill Amo more, especially when it was obvious the big dumbass didn't recognize Valerie much in her new clothes, but he should've known he had nothing to worry about with Amo. His arrogance would get himself in trouble.

"Easy, doll." Amo finally recognized her from earlier in the underground. "I don't want to kick your ass and make you feel bad."

"You know what? Be my guest," Sal offered gleefully, opening the door wide when he saw those fighting words lighten Valerie's eyes.

It was quick and dirty with multiple KOs before Amo had enough of getting his ass kicked and handed off the controller to the next lucky player. As she kicked the men's asses one by one, Angel, Nero, and Dominic had their fair share against her, but not one of them came out victorious.

It wasn't until Katarina gave her best shot against Valerie that someone stood a chance, even though it was *slight* by KOing Valerie once.

With only few of them left to try to best her, a controller was held out for Vincent to take.

"No, thanks."

Amo nudged his friend. "Come on, man."

"I said, *no, thanks*," Vincent repeated, making himself clearer.

Trying her best to move the awkwardness of the situation, Maria raised a brow at her brother. "Lucca, then?"

Lucca wrapped an arm behind Chloe's back, clearly enjoying the show and comfortable where he was. "That's all right. I'll save myself the embarrassment."

"One man standing." Kat's smile turned into a wicked sneer from excitement. "Go on, Sal."

"Oh, this will be good." Amo grabbed the popcorn from in front of Valerie for himself. she had asked for a snack to keep up her energy to kick their asses, and it was now being passed around for the others to enjoy as they witnessed history. The oooing and ahhing continued as Sal took the controller, ready to face off in a battle of bloody guts and glory.

This match didn't go down like the others, where Valerie had triple KO'd each one of them. They started out the gate in a rare tie with everyone's eyes glued to the TV.

Scared to get beaten, or to win, he knew he'd never hear the end of it either way, knowing either the guys would make jokes that a girl was finally able to beat The Great Salvatore or Valerie would accuse him of cheating like she had last night in Mario Kart.

It was a lose-lose situation; under no circumstances was Sal coming out of this a winner.

VALERIE WIPED THE SWEAT OFF HER FOREHEAD WITH the inside of her elbow. Fucking hell, he was good, but she'd be damned if he ended her winning streak.

"What the hell do you do?" Amo asked, looking at Valerie in disbelief when they went to another tie.

"She designs video games," Kat said appreciatively.

"Well, that explains the nerd-off," Amo huffed, watching them go at it. "You're not able to look up our Internet history, too, are you?"

Thankfully, Valerie laughing didn't cost her the game when she realized how it was that Sal put the fear in the big men. "I don't really use my gifts for that. I more so use them on myself."

"Someone could learn something from her, *ahem*"— Amo coughed loudly—"Sal."

"What do you mean by that?" Sal asked, responding to Valerie and not the annoying cougher.

"Like, I mostly just incognito my shit." She shrugged between mashing the buttons. "For instance, you probably *tried* searching me up, huh?"

Sal's heart dropped as she continued on, knowing full well he had.

"Then all you found were some speeding and parking tickets, and I'm sure you found out that I'm broke."

His silence made all of their mouths drop, hanging on to her every word while they simultaneously watched the screen.

"Well, that's not news to anyone." Valerie laughed, uncaring that she was airing out her business. "The trick is you keep that stuff for show 'cause *no one's* squeaky clean."

Fucking hell, that was smart. He had to admit he hadn't

bothered to try to look into her deeper, taking the surface level as good enough.

"That's why I left my speeding tickets, 'cause, I mean, who the hell pulls someone over and gives them a ticket for going eleven over?"

Sal, still dumbfounded he hadn't thought of that, tried his best to take in this new information all while trying to murder her in the game.

"You got a speeding ticket for going eleven over?" Vincent ended his vow of silence there, getting pissed. "That's foul."

"Well, technically, I was going ten over. I know 'cause I had my cruise control set for it. I thought going ten over was an unspoken rule for being okay."

"Nah, it's five," Amo told her, popping another kernel into his mouth.

"Ten," Kat visibly disagreed, making Dominic give his baby sister a scolding look.

"*Five.*"

"Ten," Maria corrected her husband.

"Agreed," Adalyn and Angel chimed in.

"Five is always a safer bet," Elle said, but her boyfriend challenged, "You shouldn't have gotten pulled over for that. That's just a waste of everyone's time."

Chloe even gave her two cents, agreeing with Nero. "I do think it was a little harsh to give you a ticket for that."

"What do you think?" Valerie asked Sal curiously, having heard the other's responses.

"I mean, you did *technically* get a ticket for *eleven*, not *ten* ri—Ow!" Sal bellowed when Maria's heel hit him in his foot.

Valerie just rolled her eyes, not sure why she thought he would think any differently than analytically. *Typical.*

Lucca, who had been quietly listening to everyone discuss, finally gave his opinion on the matter. "Do you know the officer's name who wrote you the ticket?"

By the dark look on his face, he meant to do something about it. She knew she was risking a man's life, but she just couldn't help it, remembering when she was almost shoved to the ground.

"Why, yes, I do—Officer Dunbar."

MARIA HITTING HIM AGAIN, THIS TIME MORE discreetly, had Sal taking a mental note of that name. He'd been on duty the night of Valerie's arrest and usually patrolled with Officer Daniels. However, he was certain if Daniels was there, she wouldn't have gotten a ticket in the first place, let alone been pulled over for that. Dunbar enjoyed giving out tickets; he had one of the highest quotas in the precinct.

Amo's big mouth spoke up again when Valerie was just about to win. "Come on; aren't you supposed to be The Great Salvatore, or what?"

Oh shit.

THE CONTROLLER SLIPPED FROM VALERIE'S HAND IN pure shock, letting Sal use his finishing move and defeating her. Thinking maybe she hadn't heard Amo correctly, she knew she actually had when Maria spoke.

"Wait—" The blonde looked around to see it wasn't only her who was confused. "You didn't even at least tell her who you are?"

"No ..." Sal gave Amo a threatening glance.

"Well, I didn't know!" he blurted out, trying to desperately save his ass. "Maybe she doesn't even know what it means. It's not like everyone's heard of The Great Salvato—"

"Oh, I think she knows." Katarina could see the obvious, just like everyone else in the room. "I think she's broken."

Valerie stood catatonic. Everything made sense as the last piece of the Sal puzzle filled itself in. *Holy fuck*, he didn't even try to *hide* his identity. How stupid could she be?

"You're The Great Salvatore?" she asked, still in disbelief but able to form words at last.

"Yep, she knows," Amo said, setting the popcorn down and getting up to leave. "Time to go."

"Oh, I think it's time for *everyone* to leave," Valerie made herself clear, staring Sal down.

"Good idea." Maria hurried for the door next.

"Goodbye."

"See ya next time."

"We had fun!" a different guest chimed in, as they all knew their stay had reached to the over-welcomed part.

With a quiet room, her eyes had yet to move from him. "I can't believe you didn't tell me that at least."

She wanted to feel hurt that he had yet to trust her with a thing, considering she had freely told him everything about her. She had hidden no part of herself and become so vulnerable with absolutely nothing in exchange. But right now, it wasn't hurt that she felt ...

"Go on." Sal sat down on the couch, preparing himself for all the questions. "Ask me everything you want to know."

Every now and then, The Great Salvatore would do a

stunt the whole world would hear about, but curiosity wasn't what she was feeling, either.

"I don't want to know how you did anything."

"You don't?" he asked, confused.

"I already know," she revealed, like what he did wasn't hard. "Why *wouldn't* I know?"

"Oh, well, okay. No reason," Sal said, not wanting his words to step himself into a pile of shit that would have him never getting laid again. "Then how come you haven't cared to look me up or stop me?"

Considering Valerie did know how he had done it, technically, she could do those things. But what Sal lacked to understand was how she could wield the power and yet had decided against using it for any personal gain.

And there was only one good explanation for that.

"Because I just want to create video games."

It was a simple and humbling answer that Sal respected her for.

"Well, that's good ... But ..." He went back to looking slightly confused. "But why does it look like you want to ask me something?"

"'Cause I do." She was glad to finally be able to express her true feelings. "Do you wanna fuck?"

WHO IS THAT?

The knock on the door didn't even have their lips coming off the other as they kissed like they hadn't already slept with each other three times in less than twenty-four hours. It wasn't until another incessant knock that Sal gave up and went for the door, certain that whoever was on the other side wasn't going to stop until he did.

Thinking it was probably Kat, since she had left her PlayStation behind, he opened the door, just to quickly try and shove it right back in place, but the person on the other side wasn't letting it go.

"Sorry, you can't come in."

The struggle at the door even had Valerie going for her bat.

"Bro, what the fuck!" could suddenly be heard through the crack until a tatted palm finally appeared, leveraging the door enough to open it.

Matthias stood there in all his glory. The playboy had officially arrived late to the party, and it was time to pay up.

"I'm going to let that slide ..." Matthias said cooly, but

then he noticed the lack of people. "Bro, did I miss the party?"

"Yep, goodbye." He hated to continue being so rude to his half-brother. He was not as close to that side of the family as he would have liked yet, but they were getting there with time.

"*Wait*," Matthais stopped him again, his gaze sliding behind Sal. He nodded his head seductively to the other person in the room. "Whose Harlequin?"

He's not that much of my brother. So, he decided to slam the door right in his face before the devil could get in. "None of your fucking business."

"WAIT! DO YOU WANT TO BE IN A VIDEO GAM—" Valerie yelled out, but it was too late, as the door became bolted. At first, she thought Angel had come back, but since she wanted to use him as a muse, she had saved some of his tattoos to memory, planning to add them to her game. That was what made her realize that it couldn't be him when the tattoos had switched sides. This one was a mirroring twin.

And while Maria had divulged a lot of information to her tonight, she didn't recall her mentioning her twin brothers.

"Wasn't that your brother?" she asked, concerned for Matthias' face, afraid his nose might have been broken in the action.

Unconcerned, his voice came out in a displeased snarl, "Why are you asking him to model for your game?"

Valerie had to hide her smile; she didn't want him to find out she liked the jealous streak in him. There wasn't a thing Sal had to worry about after finding out everything she had learned about him tonight. She had no plans of letting a diamond slip through her fingers. A natural diamond could only be created under immense pressure, and they were about as rare as a blue moon.

She tried to lure him upstairs. Truthfully, her mind had been made up upon seeing his computer setup, anyway, but finding out that he was The Great Salvatore was definitely the icing on the cake.

Now, it was time to eat it.

"Every video game developer uses models. It's not as big of a deal as you think it is. Besides"—she gave him an appreciative look—"I think I want to make you one of the lead characters in my next one."

He brought her face closer to his for a kiss, all jealousy suddenly wiped away and replaced with need. "That so?"

"Mmhmm," Valerie cooed, staring into his blackish-blue orbs. They held so much depth, more depth than she had ever thought possible. They not only matched her hair, but his soul, and in that moment, she knew they were meant as a pair.

As if he sensed the difference in her thoughts, Sal went to pull back. "Did Maria tell you anything?"

Blinking, Valerie had no idea what to say. Did she lie or tell the truth? Then, if she did, how much of it did she tell him she knew of his story?

"She did."

Sal understood the unspoken words. Valerie couldn't help but look at him differently, to see him as he was completely, besides just being The Great Salvatore. Instinctively, Sal knew that look all too well.

"How much did she tell you about me?"

"Enough," Valerie finally admitted. There was no lying to the man who held all the secrets.

"I see." Sal moved away from her in that instant, and she hated the look he held in his eyes. Even when she tried to explain that Maria had only done so as a sister, that look of sadness never changed. He just stood there, staring out through the floor-to-ceiling windows and up to the almost full moon.

She only wished she could read his thoughts.

"I know you might be hurt, but I am glad she told me. You keep everything so hidden and locked away so tightly that it's hard to even see you, Sal."

"That's how I've always liked to keep it," he admitted, finally speaking in a soft tone. "Because I don't like it when people look at me the way you are now."

"How do you think I'm looking at you?" she questioned and got her answer quickly.

"In pity."

"You think I'm looking at you in pity?" Valerie said confusedly. If that was the case, he needed to look at her again.

Turning his face from the moon, he made sure his eyes met hers. It wasn't often Valerie turned serious, because life was too short and way too serious for her liking, but when she did, she meant every word.

"This is me looking at a man I think I could actually fall in love with. A man I think could break my heart. A man who could hurt me and toss me aside like he did with the other women before me. I'm not looking at you 'cause I feel sorry for you, Sal. I'm looking at you because, for the first time since I got thrown out by my father, another man is gaining the power to be able to do that very same thing to me again."

THOSE WORDS STRUCK SAL RIGHT IN HIS HEART.

Valerie possessed a vulnerability he had never had. When you looked at her, you could see her for all she was. There was nothing about her that was *hidden and locked away* like she had said about him. Hiding who he was, was his way of shielding himself from the rest of the world, which was ironic considering the rest of the world could never be hidden from him. How could he possibly be upset that, for the first time in his life, a woman he was interested in had to see him for all that he was worth? It was something he had been fearful of his whole life—to be vulnerable with a woman and let her in on all his secrets. But what was he supposed to do? Keep them hidden forever? Or finally let someone have a peek at him out from behind the computer screen?

"I got lucky my father wanted nothing to do with me." He started letting down his firewalls as he spoke, knowing it was all Valerie was asking. He had already made his decision in wanting her, so it was time to admit Maria might have done him a favor tonight. It was left up to him if he wanted to lose her or let her in. "I got the best end of the deal out of all my siblings. Dominic, Angel, Matthias, Katarina, and Cassius had it much worse than I ever did, even when I was living on the street. I simply didn't really know Lucifer, only that he was a person to fear and stay away from. My brothers and sister were the ones who had to deal with him, and while I have hate in my heart for Lucifer for other things he has done, I don't have hate in my heart for him as my father. 'Cause he wasn't one to me. He's still alive to this day, rotting away, but I refuse to see him, to give him the satisfaction to think I thought he was my father 'cause he wasn't."

Valerie's shock was apparent when he first started to

speak of his own father, but that shock was replaced with a different kind of shock from this new knowledge.

"Lucifer is still alive?"

"Yes," Sal said, knowing it was impossible for Maria to have told her everything. He could sugarcoat things for her, but his life and profession were impossible to sweeten. "He's waiting for his executioner to wake up."

"And who is that?" she asked, her mouth going dry.

"The son he managed to kill the most inside," Sal revealed, and little did she know it was the one she had just briefly met. "Matthias."

STICKY SITUATION

"Are you sure you'll be okay by yourself for thirty minutes?"

"It's not like I'm going to run away." Valerie stopped her packing to see that he wasn't fully convinced, even after last night.

They hadn't spent the night bickering or having sex. They had spent it talking about not only their past but their hopes and dreams, too. Sal opening up about Lucifer had only been the beginning, and while she hadn't learned everything there was to know about Sal yet, in time, she would.

"Listen, I promise you're stuck with me until either I go to prison or your dick gets sick of me, okay?"

The smirk that played on Sal's lip lasted only for a moment. "Okay, I'll be next door, picking up a few things. I'll be right back."

She shooed him to go on as she continued her packing.

Having only just started, Sal was convinced he easily had thirty minutes to get next door and to get in and out.

It wasn't that Sal was afraid of her being a flight risk

anymore. He was afraid about how unpredictable she was. He was unable to convince her not to take her bat with them, because she thought riding with a made man meant she needed to be "strapped" at all times, and there was no telling her that was what his gun was for. In this sticky situation, he decided on waiting to tell her that he was the one who actually had her computer all along until he could get her weaponless and preferably in a padded safe room.

After unlocking his front door and entering his house, he made sure the blinds were firmly shut from Valerie's prying eyes and sat down at her computer, wanting to give it a deeper look now that he knew she was capable of incognito'ing her shit. Sal wasn't doing it for his usual prying reasons, certain Valerie was the girl for him; he was doing it in case he had missed something to help her case. Then, if he was really lucky and quick, he might be able to play a couple of rounds of Bubblegum Blitz.

It had taken longer for Valerie to pack her drinks, snacks, and candy than her clothes. Finishing in record time, she loaded her things into Sal's car, convinced that there was no way she could talk him into taking her car again. When he had still yet to come out of his place, she went up to his front door, contemplating going in. Thinking she might never get the chance again to see inside his house, she barged in ... only to find a sight she thought she'd never see.

With her jaw dropping to the ground and anger seething in part of her every being, it was worse than witnessing Sal sleeping with another woman.

Much ...

Much ...
Worse.

"WHAT THE FUCKITY FUCK DO YOU THINK YOU'RE doing?"

Only catching the end of her screams when the headphones were snatched off his head, Sal whipped around in his chair to see Valerie standing right behind him.

"I—" Making sure she wasn't holding her bat, Sal regretted not having a wireless headset and could only hope that she wouldn't use the wire to strangle him to death. "Valerie, I can explai—"

"Oh, you can, can you?" She threw down his headset in a brazen fury, breaking it.

Welp, at least she didn't plan on strangling him, *so that's a plus.*

"Please fucking explain to me why it is you're playing *my* game, on *my* computer that you have conveniently let me believe the police have been holding hostage this whole time!"

With each word being shrieked out louder than the last, Sal held out his hands, officially fearing for his life. "Listen, maybe when you calm down, I can—"

"*Calm down?*"

Her voice shrilled to an auditory level that Sal never thought was possible, causing his eyes to slam shut. Anticipating more of her wrath, he squinted his eyes open to find that she had spun on her heels and was walking right back out his front door.

Fuck, fuck, fuck!

"Come on, Valerie. Please, you know Lucca will kill me

if I let you leave. We can talk about this." Following behind her at a safe distance had been his second mistake, thinking she had just planned on leaving when she actually went to slide her bat from out of her car. "Holy shit, Valerie!"

Pointing the bat a centimeter away from his face, she suddenly looked eerily calm. Sal didn't like that look, not one bit.

"As much as I'd love to add a murder charge onto my ongoing record, I think I'll take your advice and let the Boogieman take care of that for me."

That was the last time he planned to give her any ideas.

Only brave enough to approach when the bat was gone from his face and she was in her car, he tried opening the driver's side door she had just disappeared into. His hand flew off the handle in a rush after she had already locked the doors. With the car starting and being put in *Reverse*, he hit her driver's side window, begging while trying to be careful not to bust the glass on her. "Don't do this, Valerie! We can talk this out!"

He went for the keys in his pocket; his last resort was to follow her in his car, but his hand reached the end of the material and came up empty. "Fuckity fuck!" he screamed at the top of his lungs, knowing Valerie must've swiped the keys off him during her tirade.

Far enough down the street away from him, she finally rolled down her window to give him the bird. "That's right, motherfucker!"

Losing his own temper, Sal held up two of his own fingers, flicking off the back of her car, hoping she'd catch it in her rearview mirror.

Her honking the horn of her Scion XB over and over again as she went down the street told him that she had gotten the message.

He contemplated pulling his gun out to shoot out one of the tires on her ugly-ass car but decided against it when he caught sight of his neighbor across the street with her mouth dropped open in stupor while holding her baby on her hip.

Sal politely waved over at her. "Hey, Katie. Beautiful day, isn't it?"

WITH NOWHERE TO GO IN THE CITY THAT SHE WAS forcibly contained to, as she was currently only out on bail, she needed help. And there was only one person who could rationally calm, let alone give her any sane advice with how she should move forward, and she hadn't been able to contact him due to her situation.

After going to a party one of her coworkers had thrown when she first got hired, it had not only been her first party experience but also the last. She was already regretting heading in that direction, but it was the only place she knew to go.

Making a right on the next street, she adjusted her rearview mirror just to be sure he wasn't following her. She did technically have his keys in her pocket, but a girl had to be certain.

Positive she couldn't possibly be followed, Valerie turned into the neighborhood, hoping her memory was correct. When she spotted the vomit-green door, she pulled into the driveway, still not able to forget the first time she had seen the hideous color.

Valerie adored color, but when men tried to do absolutely anything with color, they always picked the worst fucking shades. Heaven forbid they ever asked a woman's opinion before they did anything. It was actually her biggest gripe with Apple.

Hey, Apple, have you ever actually seen the color pink?

Turning her car off, she exited it and walked right up to the door, knocking loudly. She thought she might've gotten unlucky and that he wasn't home, when the door flung open.

"Valerie?"

"Hey, Lyle." She wasted no time letting herself in. "I need you to get in contact with someone for me."

"Wait a second." Lyle still had his headset on and Xbox controller in his hand, clearly taken off guard. "I thought you were in prison?"

"No, not yet. I'm out on bail at the moment," she clarified, trying to get this going. "So, can you help me out or not?"

"Okay, sure," he finally agreed with the shake of his head. "How can I help?"

"Where's your gaming PC?"

Scratching the back of his head, he tried to laugh it off. "I don't have one at the moment. I just have an Xbox."

What a noob. Rolling her eyes in disgust, she held out her hand out for the Xbox controller, finding it sticky.

Ew.

She looked around at this bachelor pad; it was totally different than the bachelor pad Sal had. *Dammit,* maybe he wasn't only the best of the bunch by made men standards, but men in general.

Valerie sat down on his couch in front of his TV, planning to burn the clothes she was wearing later. Moving the controller sticks with her thumbs, she quickly wrote Justice a message through Xbox, telling him it was urgent and to contact her on this account ASAP. Hoping it would make it to Justice's PC account, she hit *Send*.

"What do we do now?" Lyle asked.

Valerie set the dirty controller down, being sure to rub the stickiness off on her pants. "Now, we wait."

"Okay." Taking an awkward seat next to her, Lyle finally took off his headset. "So, what do you want to do until then?"

"I want you to stay on that side of the couch"—she made herself clear at seeing the hopeful possibilities swirling in his mind—"and order me a pizza."

RELEASE THE KRAKEN

Having eaten the whole pie by herself, Valerie sat back on the couch full as she watched Lyle gun down someone in Fortnite.

"Ha-ha, you bitch!" Lyle screamed into the headset to a probably fourteen-year-old kid. "That's right; go cry to your mommy."

Having seen enough, Valerie just shook her head, then went into his kitchen for a drink. While Lyle's taste in video games sucked, he at least had good taste in drinks when she pulled a cold blue Powerade from his fridge.

Valerie quenched her thirst; she hadn't had one of these bad boys in days. She wondered when Justice would finally reach out. If he didn't get a hold of her soon, she was about to take her chances and go on the run to Texas to find him in person.

About to seriously give up when she heard Lyle yelling at a girl player to go back in the kitchen and make him a sandwich, a knock could be heard on the door.

Peeking her head back into the living room, she gave Lyle a look of death. "Who is that?"

Lyle stopped playing a moment to look at her then shrugged. "I don't know."

Valerie's eyes turned into slits, smelling bullshit, and it wasn't his dirty underwear that was lying about. "Did you tell anyone I was here?"

"No—"

"Who did you tell?" she whisper-screamed at him, knowing instantly that he was lying through his fucking unbrushed teeth. "Tell me right now, or so help me God, Lyle, that'll be the last fucking game you play on your Xbox ever again."

It wasn't until she was about to rip the console out of its place that Lyle finally gave in.

"Fine! I might have told Gerald that you're here."

Gerald was another one of their coworkers, but when another knock came at the door, this time louder, she began threatening him with her hands still on the Xbox.

"Tell me exactly what you said. *Word for word.*"

"All I said was that he wasn't going to believe who was here, and then I told him it was you." He added the last part in a rush after she had ripped out its cords and looked like she was about to drop it. "I swear that's all!"

She was contemplating throwing the stupid thing to the ground and smashing it to tiny bits when Lyle stood up and went for the door.

"It's not a big deal. I'm sure Gerard just came over to say hi—"

"No! Do not open the door!" she screamed out when her gut told her that something was wrong, but it was too late as a bullet went right through Lyle's face. It was much different in real life than in her video games. It was certainly a lot messier and strangely a lot quieter than she had expected, due to the silencer on the end of the barrel of the gun.

Splattered in blood and knowing that her time had come, Valerie had nothing to lose. And, frankly, Lyle didn't either, considering he was dead, so she chucked the Xbox she still had in her hands right at the fully covered intruder. Having knocked them senseless, Valerie ran as fast as she could to her car and shut herself in before starting it.

"Shit!" she cried out when she found her keys no longer sat in the ignition. Whoever had come in to kill her had been thorough in giving her no possibility of escape, which led her to no other option but ...

She eyed her bat in the passenger seat. The bitch had fucked up by leaving it in her car. She made a promise that *that* was going to be the last mistake he would ever make.

Gripping her bat as she exited the car, she prepared to fight to the death when the masked assailant rushed out of the house at the same moment. Once he caught sight of her, Valerie ran right at him, holding her bat high in the air as he pointed the gun right at her.

Bang! Bang! Bang!

The blood that coated Valerie this time, she wasn't sure if it belonged to her or not. It didn't feel like she had gotten shot, and she certainly hadn't been the one to fall to the ground.

"Are you fucking stupid?" a masculine voice roared from behind her.

Turning to see Officer Daniels with his gun still smoking out from the barrel, she dropped the bat, still in shock, and realized that she wasn't dead and dreaming. "Huh?"

"I said, *are you fucking stupid?*" he roared at her again,

but she was only barely able to catch it over the ringing in her ears.

"Well, what the hell was I supposed to do?" she asked snarkily, trying to calm her heart rate down from almost being killed. "Let him kill me without a fight? No, thanks!"

"No," he said harshly, looking at her as if she were fucking crazy. "You were supposed to run the *other* way!"

"And let him shoot me from behind?" She picked her bat back up and swung it over her shoulder. "Again, no, thanks."

For both of their safeties, Officer Daniels put his gun back in its holster.

While grateful to still be alive, Valerie gave him a curious look. "How'd you know this was happening, anyway?"

"I followed you—"

"Well, that's not creepy at all," Valerie had his words coming to a halt.

"Fucking hell, woman, a *thank you for saving my ass* wouldn't hurt." When he knew he wasn't going to get that, as she kept staring at him to continue his story, he did. "After Sal found your house ransacked, he asked if I could keep a patrol out on your neighborhood."

"Oh, so, it wasn't the police who broke all my shit ..." She understood now. Obviously, since Sal hadn't mentioned that he had her computer, he couldn't tell her that it wasn't the police who had trashed her home.

"No." Unimpressed, he continued, "So, when you left the neighborhood in your little blaze of glory earlier today, I happened to be nearby, and he asked me to tail you."

Slightly embarrassed he had witnessed that, and that she absolutely sucked at making sure no one was following her, she twirled her bat in her hand. "I see. So, he knows I've been here this whole time …?"

"Yes." He nodded at her pityingly. "He asked me to keep an eye on you till you hopefully cooled down and came to your senses."

If Valerie thought she could get away with using her bat on Officer Daniels, she would. But she was almost positive it wouldn't go as well as it had on Sal.

"So, if you've been watching me this whole time, then how the hell did you almost let me die?"

"Because I got called off scene. The only reason I came back in time was because your boyfriend must've been tracking me and forced me to come back."

Ah … While she wasn't sure she and Sal were on boyfriend/girlfriend terms yet, having a *friend* in the mafia who was also conveniently good with computers definitely had its perks. Hence, while she was still extremely pissed at Sal, she was a bit less furious with him now.

"What does he have on you?" she finally asked after not only seeing but hearing the disdain in his voice.

"That's between me, God, and The Great Salvato—"

"You know I can easily look it up, too, right?" She gave him her own pitying gaze.

"Fine," Daniels grumbled, giving in. "I fucked Sheriff Calloway's wife, but that was only because he's fucked over half the women in the precinct."

Valerie simply shrugged, finding it completely understandable. "Oh, okay."

Officer Daniels just laughed.

When he wouldn't stop throwing his head back in laughter, she looked at him strangely. "What's so funny?"

"The fact that I've been worried sick about you in the hands of the Carusos. But something tells me you fit right in." He approached the dead body on the ground and gave it a turn. "Actually, I think you might be safer with them."

Considering her predicament, *that was probably true.*

"Do you know him?" Daniels asked after removing the ski mask.

"Yeah, some idiot from work." Valerie hated to speak ill of the dead, but it was the truth. "His name's Gerard."

"And who's that?" he asked, pointing to the dead guy at the door.

"Lyle. An even bigger idiot." She didn't even bother to look at her other deceased coworker and instead bent over to go through Gerard's pockets. Frankly, what was done was done. "There are my car keys."

"Valerie ..." He watched her dumbfoundedly. "Why does he have them in the first place?"

At that point, Valerie held up her hand. She had heard enough from the male species in one day. "Don't ask."

"Here you go."

Sal caught the keys Officer Daniels had thrown his way, looking down at them to see they were Valerie's.

"I didn't think you'd want her to get away again. It almost cost me an unmarked car. But, thankfully, I *felt* when she lifted the keys off me."

"Thanks," Sal said, clearing his throat of embarrassment. As much as it hurt for Sal to do, he held out his hand for the man to properly thank him this time. "Thank you, Officer Daniels."

Daniels took the strong hand in his, knowing it meant a truce between the two. "No problem."

"If you need *anything*, just let me know," Sal said the words, knowing he understood them perfectly.

"Same to you," he agreed before he had to clarify, "As long as it doesn't involve Valerie Monroe. *That*, you'll have to get the Caruso soldiers to take care of next time."

"All right," he agreed to happily with a laugh.

He'd noticed that Valerie had caught Officer Daniels' attention; it had been the only explanation as to why he hadn't wanted to hand over her computer, but he was happy that Valerie had forced that ship to sail. Sal didn't like being jealous. After being jealous of everything anyone had for the first thirteen years of his life, he no longer wanted to feel that feeling. And he especially didn't like being jealous of a jacked cop in a uniform.

"Listen, I had to use Valerie's computer to track you. I just wanted to be sure that won't cause her any trouble."

"No, I don't think so." He shook his head. "My bet is Gerard was the one to frame her, so I expect her charges to be dropped in the morning."

"Sounds good."

"How'd you get here, anyway?" he asked Sal, knowing he had been stranded at the house.

"I might have jacked my neighbor's car," he admitted without remorse, giving him back a different set of keys from his pocket. Why every woman on Prairie Drive thought their neighborhood was so safe from carjacking was beyond him. "Is there any way you could take it back to Katie, our neighbor across the street, and let her know the situation? I think it might be better coming from a cop than out of her thieving neighbor's mouth."

"Sure. Anything else?" He laughed, sensing there was.

"There is another thing ..." The request Sal was about

to ask for was highly different than the last. "It's about Officer Dunbar."

Daniels crossed his arms over his chest. "What about him?"

"He gave a speeding ticket to Valerie a few months back."

Confused as to where this was going, he didn't understand. "What am I supposed to do about that—"

"It was for eleven over," Sal revealed, and in that instant, even Daniels' face couldn't hide his disbelieve at the weak number. "So, either *you* lower your partner's expectation of the people of Kansas City, or *I* will."

"I'll see what I can do," Daniels told him, getting the message on behalf of his partner's sake. "You sure you can handle it from here?"

Sal took a deep breath before giving a nod, having only one thing left to do.

"Shall I release the Kraken?" the officer asked, just to be sure.

It had been awfully quiet the last ten minutes, and he could only hope the monster had tired itself out. "Go ahead."

However, he should have known he wasn't going to get that lucky when Officer Daniels opened the back of his unmarked cop car, and a trapped Valerie jumped out with a vengeance.

"You motherfuckers."

BAGGED MYSELF A BOYFRIEND

"**Y**ou *bob*, and then you *weave*, Valerie!" Sal scolded her, taking his hand off the steering wheel to show her what he meant by making a zigzag motion. "I don't understand how you play video games and don't know that."

"I know that," she muttered under her breath with her arms crossed over her chest.

"Then you certainly should fucking know that you don't bring a goddamn Harlequin cosplay bat to a gunfight!"

"Why the hell am I getting ridiculed right now? I almost died, and you're the one who's been lying to me this whole time!"

"Exactly. You almost died. Thankfully, I saved your ass in time because I had your computer in the first place. So, I'm pretty sure that gives me a pass."

Valerie went to open her mouth to say something smart but had absolutely nothing to say because, frankly, he was right.

"Still hurt you did that, though, especially after last

night." Her voice revealed just how much he had hurt her; they both knew he'd had plenty of opportunities to tell her.

"Listen." Sal softened his voice a tad but still held a bit of firmness. "Real life isn't anything like video games. You can't respawn after you die. I'm only telling you this"—his jaw flexed a bit—"because I care about you, Valerie. So much so that I let a lie by omission get out of hand 'cause I didn't have the balls to tell you the truth. Then you did the exact thing I was afraid you'd do by running away."

Valerie no longer held her arms so tightly across her chest. Instead, she loosened them, placing her hands in her lap and feeling awful for leaving him like that. Just how she had fears of him leaving her already, he did, too.

"I'm sorry. I sometimes let my temper get a bit out of hand."

"*A bit?*"

At feeling a sense of rage come up, she had to bite it down not to prove his point. "Maybe a little *more* than a bit." She had to say the words with a clenched jaw after she quickly remembered that he had said he cared about her. Then, if that wasn't enough, she had seen another bachelor's way of life, making her even more certain after today that Sal was the man for her. "I care about you, too."

Sal took his hand off the wheel to take hers in his and held it firmly. "I haven't let myself care about anyone like this *ever*. I'm afraid of getting attached to someone only to have them ripped away from me. It took me three years before I let myself accept the Carusos as my family. I was too afraid they'd change their minds and throw me back out on the street. I understand the thoughts in my brain aren't healthy. It will take some time before I ever believe you won't leave me."

"I don't plan on leaving you again." Her grip held his back tighter in a promise.

While they had talked about his past last night, he hadn't mentioned those kinds of thoughts and feelings for her yet, also revealing both of them had a fear of abandonment due to their own issues. She supposed it was only another reason Sal had joined the mafia. Giving his oath to the family meant he'd have one for life.

"If you don't want me to, of course."

"I'll never be able to control my thoughts on your safety," he warned, letting her know that he didn't have plans to let her go, either. "A made man will always worry about his girl's safety."

His girl, she replayed the words, looking down at their intertwined hands in disbelief. No one had ever held her hand before, let alone make her their girl. Certain she had just gotten her first boyfriend, she'd be sure to iron out the details later.

Right now, only one thing came to her mind as butterflies fluttered in her stomach. "Are we going back to the house?"

He seemed unsurprised by her sudden change in subject, so he had obviously grown used to her focus level.

"Yes, your stuff is still in my car, and I don't exactly enjoy driving this shit box," he reminded her of her little key stint.

"The Casino Hotel is closer, though," she couldn't help but mention.

"I thought you might want your computer back." Sal looked at her in confusion. Maybe not wanting her clothes, he could understand, but not wanting her computer back was practically unbelievable.

"I suppose the car could suffice ..." she said, looking at

the back seat. While it was rather tiny on the outside, her car was a bit of a clown car with the inside more spacious than you'd think.

Sal took his eye off the road to look over at her.

"Suffice for what?"

"To fuck."

VALERIE RAN HER HAND LOVINGLY OVER HER PC. "I have missed you so much. Come to Mama."

She loaded up her game; it wasn't hers, but it would do in a pinch. She had been playing for five minutes when she saw the notification of a name pop up as they were entering the game.

"What's up, Justice?" she squealed through her headset. "I've missed you. Have you missed me?"

"Yeah, I really missed losing to you. My ranking went higher. I have to admit it did dull the pain."

"If I weren't so happy to have my computer back right now, I would be hurt," she said, placing a hand over her heart as if he could possibly see it.

"You going to tell me what happened? I've been waiting for you to get online and find out."

"You still haven't gotten my message? I sent you one through ... well, a now deceased person's Xbox."

"Geez, we will have to get back to that." You could hear the headset practically shaking on his head before he continued. "I don't own an Xbox anymore, so I never linked my account to my PC to even receive a message from there."

Of course, he didn't. Justice had taste. With her hope restored in gamers, she began to catch him up to speed.

"My dude, I got arrested! Can you believe that?"

"I did happen to catch that," Justice reminded her of that night they had stayed up to play games. "So, what did you get arrested for? Eating too many Twizzlers? Buying too many MoonPies?"

"Bro!" Gunning him down, she raised her arm, doing a fist-pump. "I've missed kicking your ass."

"Valkyrie! What did you get arrested for?"

"For cyber-attacking the Horseshoe. Can you believe that? It's why I had to try messaging you through someone's Xbox. They confiscated my electronic devices." Valerie gave a sarcastic snort into the mic. "If I were to cyber-attack someone, I would—"

"Valkyrie!" Justice yelled. "Get your tanks!"

Concentrating on the game, she waited until she was safe before she started talking again. "Anyway, I got to meet this really hot lawyer. I'm going to make him an avatar in a new game I'm thinking about. Once I go back and put some final finishing touches on Bubblegum Blitz, that is."

"You can't use your lawyer as inspiration for an avatar."

"Why not? Did you not hear me tell you he's hot?"

Valerie pulled out a bag of Twizzlers that she had hidden from Sal. He only let her have a pack a day, spewing all these scientific facts about red dyes she couldn't care less about.

Uncaring about her taste in men, he had to put her back on track of their discussion. "When do you have to go to court?"

"If I'm lucky, never. We're hoping to have the charges dropped soon. Hey! Did I tell you my bail was two million dollars! Isn't that fucking cool?"

"Yeah, cool." Justice blasted her to smithereens, trying to keep up with her tangents. "What are you doing about playing on the Internet? Won't you get in trouble? You should get off."

"Sal let me have my computer back out of self-preservation and told me that I *shouldn't* get into any trouble for it."

"Salvatore?" he asked, like he was making sure he'd heard her correctly over the missiles she had just sent his way. "As in your next-door neighbor that you have despised with your whole being for the last six months?"

"Funnily enough, it turns out he's not a cheater ..." she admitted with fake laugher that those accusations on her part had been completely false. Valerie couldn't, however, tell him the full truth about him, either.

"Well, I don't think he was playing video games with the girls he brought home," he said in a slightly worried tone.

"Oh no, he was being a total manwhore, but it turns out that he's sweet, and kind, and really, really, really hot."

"Wow, he got three *really hot*s. You only gave your lawyer one," he quickly noted. "It sounds serious."

"Hopefully." Valerie smiled to herself. "I might've finally bagged myself a boyfriend. I'll hold out hope that you'll finally find a girlfriend soon."

"Thanks for that," Justice simply muttered. "So, can we go back to the deceased person's Xbox?"

"Oh yeah!" She remembered the important detail, trying to think back over their conversation if she had told him yet or not, since she got distracted with all the times she already killed him in the game. "Did I tell you someone was trying to kill me? Scared the crap out of me. I went to my coworker Lyle's house to try to get in contact with you. Unfortunately, he was murdered while I was there. I barely escaped with my life. Dying and fighting for your life isn't at all like the games we pla—"

"Did you tell your lawyer?" Justice's voice cut through her sentence.

"I was going to get Sal to call him in the morni—"

"I would have him text your lawyer tonight, so he can talk to the police," Again, he cut her off with a sense of urgency.

"Sal's already talked with the police. I don't think there's anything he can do about it tonight, anyway."

A frustrated sigh came through the mic after he got blown up. "Valkyrie, there has to be a reason you're being accused of cyber-stalking and why you were almost killed along with your coworker. You had to have seen or heard something you weren't supposed to know."

"I didn't. I only worked at the Horseshoe for a short amount of time. Even when I broke through their firewalls to prove a point that they needed to install a better system, I didn't see anything that raised any red flags," she told him with confidence, having already considered this a million times when she'd been held up in the cell for the long week-end. "So, why kill Lyle? And try to take me out? If I'm convicted, I'll be out of their hair, anyway."

"Because you know something ..." Justice's voice trailed off. "Or have something ..." His voice rose from pulling his mic closer to his face. "Valerie! You have something!"

Valerie had to lower the volume on her headset at his raised voice, and she found it funny when he used her real name. Yes, he knew her real name, but he had never used it before. "What would I even have?"

"How in the fuck do I know?" Justice was practically yelling at her. "Did you ever take anything from work?"

Putting a Twizzlers in her mouth, she had to think for a moment. "Maybe I shouldn't mention what I took over the Internet."

"For God's sake, think, Valkyrie. *Hard.*"

"Okay!" she yelled back, trying to do so as she mulled it over her candy. But now she was in the mood for something else since he had mentioned the word *hard*. Valerie wondered when Sal would be back from his office; he had left her safe in his penthouse to take care of a few things.

"Do you still have the stuff you took?"

His words brought her back to what she was supposed to be thinking about. "I didn't take *that* much. Let's see, a monitor, graphics card, a RAM—"

"The RAM, where is it now?" he asked with urgency, knowing that was what stored all a computer's data.

"I don't know ..." It was hard for Valerie to think now that she had Justice's avatar in her crosshairs. "It's probably gone, actually. Did I mention my house got broken into? I kept all my unused parts at home in a box in my office. The only reason they didn't get a hold of my computer was because Sal took it."

"No, that was not mentioned." Justice's voice could be heard in a growl.

"It's not like it matters, anyway. Everything that could hold memory or data, I wiped clean once I brought it home. Anything I might've taken wasn't worth taking to the scrapyard. They were older than me—" Valerie broke off, suddenly remembering something while she waited for Justice's next life to regenerate. "There was a flash drive I found a while back, though. I had actually forgotten all about it. I bet it's still in my stash of loose items I keep in the pot of a faux plant. It came with the desk, so when I got fired, I couldn't take the plant and forgot I had hidden some stuff in there."

"Where exactly did you *find* the flash drive?" he asked, sensing where this was going.

"On the floor ... in someone's office," she finally admitted.

"So, you took it," he corrected her, sighing, "Whose office was it?"

"Um ... let me think ..." Valerie shot down Justice, who was finally on his last life. She did another fist-bump in the air to celebrate. She was surprisingly on her game, considering she hadn't been playing lately.

"Valkyrie!" Justice yelled. "Quit playing and think."

"I think it was my boss' office. Edmond's ..." As she said the name, it suddenly clicked with her that those charges were not only never going to be dropped, but they were never going to let her see the inside of a courtroom. To make it worse, she didn't even have what they wanted, and she didn't know how many people were involved for certain, past Gerard, until she got the part back.

"Justice, I have to go. Thanks for the game and the help! I have to go find Sal and get him to take me to the Horseshoe. I think I left it inside the potted plant on my desk. Love ya! Bye!"

"Valkyrie! Don't go ye—"

She quickly turned off the game. She didn't have the time to explain it to Justice, whether he sounded nervous for her or not.

She had only one mission: Find Salvatore.

ONCE IN A BLUE MOON

"What the hell do you think you're doing?" Sal shot up from the chair in his office when the unannounced man barged in.

"Where's Valerie?"

He was one second away from pulling his gun out to kill the man he had a high distaste for but thought better of it, considering Valerie still might need his services. "Kent, I understand you are representing her at the moment, but you can't just barge in—"

"I don't have time to explain," Kent said, holding up his hand to silence him. "Now, where is Valerie? This is important."

"She's in my penthouse." Sal felt safe enough to divulge that information because Kent didn't know which one he lived in. The lawyer had only known this was his office because Sal took a meeting with him for personal reasons a little over six months ago.

He figured he must have heard about Lyle and Gerard and wanted to speak with Valerie, but he wasn't sure why it couldn't wait until morning, until he heard the worry in Kent's voice.

"I need you to check—right now."

Seeing just how serious the lawyer was, Sal sat back in his chair while biting down his fury, and pulled up the personal cameras in his penthouse. They were the only cameras he had access to in any of the penthouses on the top floor. Those cameras were all personally watched by their respective owners.

He flipped through them but didn't find her. She might be in the bathroom, where no camera was placed, but when he rewound the footage a bit, he realized she had actually left the penthouse.

"She's not there anymore, is she?" Kent asked gravely.

Sal shook his head, trying not to let the same worry overtake him just yet.

Quickly, he followed her tracks after leaving the penthouse, flipping through the camera viewpoints. Kent came up behind him to watch the screens, as well. Valerie had first come to his office, which made Sal's heart sink even lower.

Kent hissed at him, "Where were you?"

"I caught someone cheating at one of the tables. I went down to the casino floor to make sure with my own eyes. Look." Sal put a split screen of the two cameras in each of the elevators. When she hadn't found Sal in his office, she had gone straight to the elevator. At the same moment that Valerie had entered one at the top floor of the Casino Hotel, Sal had entered one at the bottom after dealing with the situation, so they rode a different one side by side. Sal had only just returned to his office when Kent barged in a few minutes later.

"That's why I couldn't get on the elevator and had to

wait so long. You both got in and must've done something to cause the elevator not to stop between floors." Kent had still been staying in one of the hotel rooms for quite some time now.

"Yes, there's a code. Fuck!" Sal cursed when he watched her try to search for him in the casino. Her search had abruptly stopped when a man came up from behind her. Sal zoomed in on the man and was able to make out the outline of the concealed gun in his pocket as they walked through the Casino Hotel.

"That was Valerie's boss at the Horseshoe, Edmond Roads," Kent told him furiously as Sal clicked on another camera angle to watch them leave through the front doors.

As she left through the front doors, she bumped into a random man with a hoodie low over his face who was returning from his jog, before Sal switched to the street camera. Fear started to overtake him as he watched Valerie cross the street toward the Horseshoe with the armed man. Alone.

"How long ago was that?" All of Kent's worry was quickly replaced by jumping into action. Both men pulled their eyes from the screens and guns from their backs as they headed for his office door and loaded the chambers.

"Five minutes ago," Sal said, slipping his gun back into its place now that it was primed.

They exited his office and entered the surveillance room with multiple screens across the wall. The newest Caruso soldier would be lucky to see the morning sun.

"Alessio, why didn't you tell me Valerie came here?"

The soldier didn't even bother to move his eyes from the screen to talk to him. "I just assumed she had found you like she said you would after I told her you were checking out a problem on the casino floor."

"You're fired." Sal's voice held authority that made the soldier finally look at him. "Immediately upon my return. Clearly, you cannot be responsible for watching surveillance if you weren't able to see that she didn't."

"We're losing time," Kent reminded him, and it took all of Sal's control not to scatter the soldier's brains all over the screens.

"Get a hold of Lucca and tell him to call in the cavalry to the Horseshoe across the street. If you manage to do that, I will spare your life. If you're lucky at all ... I won't return," he told the panic-stricken soldier, who went for his phone as they left the room to run toward the elevator.

They got on in a rush, and he saw Kent go for his phone. "Who are you calling?"

"Trying to call in more backup, but the elevator is disrupting my signal." Kent cursed, pulling the phone from his ear before he apologized unremorsefully. "No offense, but I prefer mine."

Sal stalked forward at the man, taking full offense. "No offense, but how the hell did you know Valerie was in trouble, anyway?"

"Does that really matter right now?" Kent asked seriously, highly aware of Sal's distaste for him.

The elevator numbers slowly counting down took away his attention. "Try texting," he told him, backing down, instinctively knowing they were running out of time. The Carusos were only the tip of the iceberg for the kind of connections Kent had. Despite how much Kent tried to hide from Sal, he did know his goings-on, but he was starting to feel like he was missing something.

While Sal still preferred his men to Kent's, at this point, he'd take any backup he could get; he realized how late it was, so Lucca was probably sleeping and at home with his wife and newborn twins.

Taking out his own phone, he sent a mass text out in the same chat he had texted the guys in to come get their women the other day.

AT HORSESHOE. VALERIE'S IN TROUBLE

When he saw the loading bar slowly creep along to deliver the message, he put the phone back in his pocket, hoping it would send when he got off the elevator, 'cause once that elevator opened, they both shot out like hell was on their heels.

Sal thought he was going to be sick from the nerves racking his body. This was exactly why he hadn't let himself get close to a woman—the fear of losing a woman he cared for would feel way too similar to losing his mother.

Sal had almost died after he lost his mom, practically starving himself to death. He had only let himself eat when the hunger pains had become too painful.

Watching his mother die in that way, and then proceeding to live on without her, was an indescribable pain he didn't wish on his worst enemy. Anything and everything he did after her passing, he hated himself for it because his mother wasn't alive and couldn't.

If tonight wasn't already eerie enough, it became only more so when he didn't see not one made man as they made their way through the casino. The chances of that happening were like ...

Once in a blue moon ...

The thought made chills coat Sal's body as they barged out of the casino doors, and Sal's feet came to a sudden halt when he ominously looked up at the night sky.

"What's wrong?" Kent asked, trying to see what had stopped him.

Sal's chest felt heavy with more fear, understanding the sudden eerie feeling that had overtaken him. "It's a full moon."

With the cold night air hitting his face, he couldn't manage to say that it wasn't only a full moon.

But a blue one.

"KEEP WALKING."

Valerie entered the Horseshoe with the barrel of a gun still pointed at her lower back. She didn't need to turn around to see that it was not only Edmond doing so, but that he had the weapon concealed in his coat pocket due to the lack of concern from the people in the Casino Hotel.

Since she was still phone-less, she had been looking for Sal on the casino floor when Edmond had found her. She knew it was bad to do as he asked and walk out of the safety of the Casino Hotel; however, she could smell the stench of desperation. Knowing his words—that he'd shoot to kill— were very much true, she had done as he asked, because as soon as she blew the proverbial whistle, he would do it, too. He was on the brink of having nothing to lose, regardless of if he found what he wanted from her. The only thing saving her at the moment was the fact she was following his orders. The next thing to save her would be to keep doing as she was—walking as slowly as she could get away with and praying to God that Sal would get her message.

"Faster," he said with a hard shove to her back with the pointy end of the gun.

"Okay," she gritted out in a slight bit of pain, thinking she needed to distract him into walking slower while they continued through the Horseshoe.

The casino was pretty much dead from the lack of players, probably because of the cyberattack.

"Edmond, I'm not sure what you think I hav—"

"Don't play dumb with me, Valerie. Once I realized it was missing, I've been looking everywhere for that fucking flash drive. I went through months of footage of my office only to find you picked it up right off my office floor. Unfortunately for me, I fired you the very next day. My mistake was letting you get arrested before trying to find it in your house. You can imagine my surprise when I realized it wasn't there."

"How'd you know I left it at the Horseshoe?" she asked under her breath.

"I wasn't for certain till just now."

Great.

Valerie tried to slow her gait a tiny bit more while she talked. "So, let's see if I have this right ... Obviously, the cyberattack was an inside job. I'm assuming that's why you didn't want me to update the firewalls—it would have thrown off your whole plan." She laughed mockingly for a moment. "I bet you got unlucky when the man before me decided to retire early, and I bet you only hired me as his replacement because you thought my lack of experience would mean I wouldn't care enough to want to fix the firewalls."

His silence told her she was exactly right.

"*My mistake*, however, was when I showed you my simulation. I gave you the perfect fall man."

"Bingo," he chastised her.

"I bet the only reason you needed Gerard's help was not only for him to do your dirty work, but to be the one to pull off the cyberattack. You're not smart enough to do that, but Gerard definitely was." Valerie had wondered why Gerard hadn't agreed with her in wanting to update the firewalls, but now she knew. "If I didn't take the fall, you were definitely going to let Gerard. He was a goner no matter what, huh?"

"Your time's almost up." Edmond pressed the elevator button for the floor her old office was on.

"It's not at my desk," she told him as the doors came to a close.

Keeping his gun still trained on her, Edmond stared back at her, not believing that she was telling the truth.

"I promise it's not. You think I would have kept that at my desk? If I had, you would have found it. I wasn't expecting to get fired that day, so when I was, I wasn't able to retrieve it." She snickered, really hoping she sounded convincing as the elevator doors opened to the tenth floor. If he made her get off here, she was as good as dead. "Come on, Edmond. At least give me some credit."

"Where the fuck is it, then?"

Valerie watched his hand waver over the numbers, waiting for her to tell him where she was leading them. Praying to God the man with the baby-blue eyes had heard her, she chose what could be her final resting place.

"The rooftop."

THE VITALES
TEN MINUTES EARLIER...

R unning had been the only thing he was able to do when he couldn't sleep, ever since he had found out the truth of his father.

Family.

It was a fickle word for a man who spoke the oath of the omertà. It meant that while you had a family you were been born into, you still swore that your loyalty to *The Family* came above all.

Vincent had thought himself lucky that joining the Caruso family was one and the same for him ... until he found out the devastating news that his father, Vinny Vitale, had betrayed his oath.

The Vitales had been the trusted advisers and confidants to the Caruso bosses since the creation of the family. With his father as one of the greatest consiglieres in history, he had helped broker a deal between the two feuding families, the Carusos and Lucianos. So, imagine the surprise when they had all found out that Vinny was the elusive killer One Shot who had not only taken Luciano lives, but the Carusos and, perhaps the most devastating of all, Dante's late wife and the mother to all his children, Melissa.

Now imagine how his son, Vincent, felt.

Looking at anything that reminded him of his father was hard. Looking at any other made man in the family was hard. Looking at his girlfriend, Lake, was hard. Hell, just looking at his reflection in the mirror was hard. But worst of all, looking at his bosses, Dante and now Lucca, was the hardest of all.

He should have been labeled as a betrayer and killed right alongside his father, yet he hadn't. Dante, Lucca, Nero, and everyone else in the family had shown him forgiveness, because they'd said there was simply nothing to forgive. Telling him that they themselves hadn't known the extent of Vinny's betrayal, so how could he have known? But he should have.

Vincent was dumb.

Naïve.

Talkative.

Idiotic.

Charming.

He was a funny yet endearing kind of person who joked way too much in life, *but not anymore.* Nothing in life was funny, or a joke, and he was, most of all, no longer a charming, naïve, talkative idiot who was dumb enough to miss the obvious.

Now, as he ran miles around downtown, in dangerous places, hoping for someone to give him a reason to kill, after months, his prayers had finally been answered.

So, imagine his surprise yet again to find them to be answered right in the Casino Hotel ...

∞

Valerie had been internally screaming for help as she was forced to leave the Casino Hotel, knowing Edmond had a trained gun right at her back. Without her bat or a weapon of her own, any false move meant she'd be dead. If it hadn't been for the crowded casino, she'd at least tried to fight back like she did with Gerard, but she hadn't been comfortable risking the lives of bystanders.

She'd kept her head forward while her eyes scanned the casino for anyone she knew who could help her, but with not a single made man in sight, or a customer willing to even look up from their slot machine, she'd known she was shit out of luck.

Trying to desperately think under pressure of what to do, she had devised her best plan of taking Officer Daniels and Sal's advice of running like hell. Sure, she'd probably get shot, but she'd have a better chance of it not being fatal or paralyzing her from the waist down.

As soon as she'd crossed the threshold of the Casino Hotel door's, she had planned to run, but that plan had gone to hell in a hand basket when a man in a gray hoodie, who had been drenched in sweat, bumped into her and sent the gun at her back pinching into her skin with no doubt of it going to leave a bruise.

The strong man had caught her from falling, making Valerie practically curse out loud. She would have preferred that, as it could have given her enough of an element of surprise to take the gun from Edmond. But, as the man had held her steady for only a brief moment, Valerie had caught that baby blue gaze under his low hood that was unmistakable.

Vincent.

And in that second, her gamer brain had known exactly what to do.

"Sorry."

Vincent had muttered harshly once he'd grabbed a hold of the woman to steady her. He had almost thought it was a boy at first, only deciding to catch her once he realized he was a she. He wanted a reason to fight someone, but he drew the line at women and children.

His hood had been so low from his run out in the cold that he didn't bother enough to look before he jogged through the open door. Nor had Vincent bothered to even look the woman fully in the face. It wasn't until he felt the rigid woman in his arms that he finally decided to give her a real look.

It was Valerie, the girl he had met yesterday at Sal's place. If he hadn't already met her, he would have thought nothing of the frightful look she gave him. He thought the obnoxious gamer held anything in her but fear.

He almost said her name, but then her lips mouthed a quiet word to him that made him realize something was really, really wrong.

Immediately, he picked up the strange man at her back, and his instincts let her pass right beside him as if he didn't know her. That was when he noticed the outline of a gun through the man's pocket at her back.

He walked only another foot before he turned, certain it was safe to watch them leave the safety of the Casino Hotel. He watched them carefully through the glass as they slowly crossed the street, buying himself time before he thought it was safe enough to follow behind.

Valerie Monroe was in serious trouble, but luckily for her, Vincent had been waiting for a fucking day like today.

The only problem? As he took his headphones out of his

ears, he could only hope he had understood what she had mouthed correctly ...

S AL AND K ENT ENTERED THE CASINO, TRYING THEIR best not to look suspicious as they headed for the elevators in not too much of a rush that would draw attention to them. They had no idea if Edmond was working alone or not, so they had to play it carefully. If her old boss knew he was about to be cornered, he didn't doubt, like any deranged animal, he would bite. However, knowing Valerie was running out of time with each passing minute, he slightly picked up his speed.

"Her office was on the tenth floor," Kent announced as they were almost to the elevators.

Sal nodded, not caring how Kent knew that at this point. He only knew that he somehow trusted the untrustworthy man where Valerie was concerned. He only hoped that both of their instincts were correct that she would have taken him to her old office.

Turning the corner sharply into the hallway that held the elevators, Sal ran right into a man with a gray hoodie. It wasn't until the man turned his head that Sal instantly recognized him.

"Vincent?"

"Yes," the soldier whispered back, reminding his superior to keep his voice down. "Your girl is in trouble."

That was when it clicked that Vincent had been the jogger who had run right into Valerie at the Casino Hotel.

He took a calming breath, knowing he had another soldier to help back him up. It was three against one, as far as he knew, and he liked those odds.

Vincent went back to what he was doing, watching the elevator numbers travel up floors, as he spoke quietly again. "She just got on the elevator with him. I'm waiting to see where it stops."

"They'll get off at the tenth floor, where her office used to be." Kent was the one to speak, and Sal agreed.

"I don't think so." Vincent shook his head, still staring at the numbers going up and unconcerned with who the man who was with Sal was. "I think she's leading him up to the rooftop."

"You *think*?" Kent asked furiously. "You can't think; you have to be fucking certain."

"Listen, man"—Vincent threw him a dirty look—"I had headphones in when she whispered it to me. But she's smart. She's been walking slower than a fucking snail to buy us time, so I think that's what she's doing by taking him to the rooftop—buying us more time by having to take the rooftop access. Watch—"

As the number hit nine, Sal had to agree that that sounded like her, but then it stopped at ten.

"Told you," Kent said, pushing the elevator button swiftly so another one would take them to the top.

"Wait." Vincent stopped them when the elevator began ticking away higher than ten. "See? They didn't get off. They're going to the rooftop."

All of them slid into the elevator with a sprint.

"We have to be certain, Sal," Kent told him as Sal's hand wavered over the numbers. "If we go all the way to the rooftop and she's not there, Valerie's dead."

Sal's finger slowly moved to the tenth floor, pausing when Vincent spoke.

"She went to the rooftop." His soldier was certain. "I know it."

As Valerie's life hung in the balance, Sal looked between the men, deciding who to listen to. If Vincent were Lucca, he would have never questioned him, but the soldier hadn't been the most reliable one, as Vincent had not only been the young and dumb one for quite some time, but he had been different since his father's death.

Sal knew all too well what losing a parent did to you. He himself hadn't become sane of mind until three years later. Every man in the family had cut Vincent some slack recently due to his loss, and now, here he was, supposed to take his word in order to save Valerie's life, and possibly his own ...

The blue moon ominously whispered to Sal, letting him know it wasn't only Valerie's life that hung in the balance.

Taking a deep breath, Sal made a decision.

VALERIE GOT OFF THE HIGHEST FLOOR IN THE Horseshoe. It wasn't the rooftop, but it was the closest they could get. Only a few workers in the casino had chosen to take their smoke breaks on the roof so they could smoke weed; they were unable to smoke it anywhere else due to the noticeable smell.

"I thought you vaped in the bathroom." Edmond's tone told her he was starting to reconsider believing her when they had to take the stairs for the rooftop access. Valerie needed to start doing everything in her power to start convincing him again.

"I did vape in the bathroom." That part was definitely true. She hadn't given a fuck, and it made the bathroom smell like cotton candy, anyway. "But I still would come up here from time to time to smoke with Lyle." That part wasn't true. Anyone smoking weed on a rooftop was dumb as fuck. You were simply asking for an accident by falling to your death. Upon further thought, that checked out perfectly for Lyle.

Edmond took in her wildly oversized clothes, having never seen the way she dressed outside of work before. "I should have known."

While they took the stairs of the rooftop access at slow pace, she could feel the sweat beginning to bead on her temples. She had hoped with how fucking slow she was going they wouldn't have made it this far, but as she swung open the door to the roof, she should have known she wasn't going to get that lucky.

Valerie had only been up here once, and it'd been during the day when she'd needed some fresh air. It was much different at night up here, as the cold air hit her face like needles.

Gingerly, she stepped closer to the ledge. The only reason she could see so clearly up here was because the full moon illuminated the rooftop as if it were a spotlight. She could almost swear it looked kind of blue.

Click.

The sound of the safety on the gun being disengaged was unmistakable, letting her know the severity of her current situation before Edmond had even told her.

"Time's up."

YOU SURE YOU'RE JUST A LAWYER?

lick.

"The only person whose time is up is yours, motherfucker," Sal said, pushing the barrel of his gun into the back of Edmond's skull. He would have blown his brains out sky high over the Kansas City skyline if Valerie weren't so close to the edge of the roof.

Unable to concentrate on Valerie, he could only hope his soldier wouldn't fail him, like he hadn't yet. If it weren't for Vincent, she'd be dead already—never would they have gone to the roof.

"Put the gun down, and I'll let it be quick, Edmond. If not, you'll have to answer to Lucca."

Sal knew those words were about the only thing that could put enough fear into the man to drop the gun. Edmond was out of his mind and thinking irrationally, but he was certain the man was of sound enough mind to understand that much.

"Last chance to drop the gun and meet the devil instead." Sal pressed it harder into his skull, trying to entice him into making a decision. "Or you'll be taken to a visit with the Boogieman soon."

Still afraid to pull the trigger, as it might cause Valerie to fall to her death, Sal was only going to give Edmond another moment more to decide, when the sound of a rock falling to the ground made Edmond turn his head toward it.

Using the distraction to his advantage, Sal pistol-whipped the asshole in the same moment he saw a flash of Vincent's form running for the edge of the building, toward Valerie.

Bang!

CERTAIN THE BULLET THAT WHIZZED ABOVE HER HEAD would have taken her out if it weren't for the man squishing her into the rough ground, she could have cried realizing who it was.

"Vincent! You got my messa—"

"Stay down!" Vincent ordered before leaving her.

Doing as the made man asked, she quickly knew why he had left her so suddenly when another shot rang out.

Bang!

SAL HAD ONLY LOOKED OVER TO VALERIE FOR A SECOND to make sure she was still on the roof and hadn't gotten shot when Edmond turned the gun on him. His mistake was not letting himself hit Edmond hard enough in the head, wanting him to live for the torture he was about to endure for the rest of his short life.

Looking down at his abdomen, he saw the pool of red

blood beginning to coat his white shirt under his suit jacket. The image was reminiscent of the wound his mom had suffered those many years ago under a full moon.

He lifted his eyes to the current moon as his knees dropped to the ground with one final, lasting thought that he finally understood why his mother hadn't been able to tear her eyes away from the moon as she'd died.

What a beautiful night to die.

"SAL!" VALERIE SCREAMED, RUNNING TOWARD HIS fallen body with tears streaming down her face. *"What do ...? What do I do?"* she screamed out for help, but Vincent was still beating Edmond senseless.

She needed a hero to come save Sal, and her prayers were answered as yet another man joined them on the rooftop.

"Apply pressure to the wound," Kent carefully instructed her, moving into action like he had done this only a million times before.

"Sal! Sal!" she sobbed, realizing how precious life was and that it was definitely nothing like in video games. "Is he dead?" she cried out hysterically to her lawyer. How he had gotten up here and was involved, she had no idea.

Kent turned Sal ever so slightly to check for an exit wound. "No, it went right through him. Beside it hurting like a motherfucker, he's just had the wind knocked out of him."

"How do you know?" Valerie sniffled, desperately trying to blink away the flood of tears rolling down her cheeks while his blood began to cover her hands.

"There are no major organs it could have hit there,

Valerie, I promise," he assured her, trying to make a tourniquet from ripping off the sleeves of Sal's suit jacket. "He's probably just in shock, but he should be coming around."

Valerie started shaking Sal's shoulders. "Sal! Sal!"

"I'm okay. Stop shaking me."

Valerie started crying harder, letting her head fall to his chest. "I thought you were d—"

"I thought so, too," Sal told her, opening his eyes. He looked back up at the beautiful orb in the sky. "There's a blue moon tonight."

"You're not going to die tonight because there's a fucking blue moon out!" Kent screamed at him.

"My mom told me—"

"I don't give a fuck what your mom told you. I'm not going to let you die tonight."

She felt like she was missing the importance of the moon when the three couldn't help but turn their heads to the sound of flesh hitting bones.

"What the fuck is wrong with him?" Kent asked, watching Vincent punch the obviously dead man to more of a pulp.

Valerie had played a lot of Mortal Kombat, but seeing a fatality like this happen in real life, right in front of her eyes, was eye-opening, to say the least.

"It's a long story," Sal told them. He himself was in awe watching his soldier go on proudly. It appeared Vincent seemed to think this was a better punishment than Edmond visiting the Boogieman.

"Sal, you good enough we can get the fuck off this roof?" Kent asked, reaching into his pocket to take out another magazine of bullets. "I might have created a problem retrieving the flash drive."

"Yeah, fuck—" He got up with a groan but made it to his

feet, picking his own gun back up. "Vincent, that's enough. We have bigger problems than a dead man right now."

As ordered, a crazed Vincent got off the carcass and slicked back his hair, coating the blond strands red.

Valerie couldn't help but notice the intent way a bloody Vincent was eyeing Kent's gun. "Sweet piece you have there."

Kent eyed the one Vincent took out from under his hoodie. From the expression on Kent's face, he not only wasn't going to return the compliment, but he didn't think the soldier should have one.

That thought clearly changed, however, as they heard the heavy footsteps of security men run up the rooftop escape. All three men on the rooftop went into position to block Valerie from the single door.

"Jackal, Ice, we've got company."

Valerie swung her head around, wondering who the hell Kent was talking to. When she didn't see anyone, she asked, "Who are Jackal and Ice?"

"A few buddies of mine," Kent answered as the men all pointed their weapons at the door. "Get ready."

Valerie was so terrified she closed her eyes and covered her ears as bullets rang out.

"Wraith ... we're running out of bullets," Kent announced as they waited for the next horde of security to make their way through.

"Who the hell is Wraith?" Valerie couldn't help but yell, officially having lost her hearing.

"Another buddy," Kent answered.

"How many buddies did you bring with you?"

"Last count, a couple dozen. They should be coming up behind the last of them right about ..."

More gunshots rang out, this time from inside.

"Now."

"You sure you're just a lawyer?" she asked in disbelief.

Kent gave her an amused grin as he pulled something out of his pocket. "I don't know, Valkyrie. You tell me."

Her jaw dropped as she stared at the flash drive that only one other person knew about. "Justice?"

Kent slowly nodded.

She couldn't help herself; Valerie gave the man a bear hug. When she noticed the jealous rage overtaking Sal's face, she pulled back. "You told me you were a veterinarian."

"I didn't lie, technically." He shrugged. "I've been known for putting a sick animal down when I had to."

Sal just rolled his eyes.

"Why didn't you tell me?" She smacked him on his chest. "You ass! You only brought me a single Nutty Buddy when you saw me in jail!"

Defensively, he moved away from her smacking hands. "They wouldn't have let you take them back to your cell."

Hurt, she averted her gaze from him. "Why didn't you tell me?"

"Valerie, you want to make money by building a make-believe world. I make my money by building a world where no one knows who I am."

Thinking that was one hell of a line that she needed to use in a video game, she wasn't able to be too angry after he had helped save her life.

"Thank you, Justice *and Vincent*." She gave them both a hug. "I don't know how I'll ever be able to repay you both. I thought I was a goner, for sure."

"And what am I? Chopped liver?" Sal scoffed, motioning to the bullet wound he had taken for her.

Valerie wound her arms around Sal's neck before

placing a tender kiss on his lips. "Oh, I know exactly how I plan to repay you."

"Lucca is waiting outside the front of the Casino Hotel with his men," Kent told him once they reached the casino floor of the Horseshoe with an armed escort, via a motorcycle club he represented that had currently also been staying at the Casino Hotel.

Sal had to give them credit; their weapons were putting the Caruso family's to shame as he and Vincent now stared in envy.

"How did you manage to keep Lucca outside?"

"I called and told him I had it under control and to keep his men back, that I wasn't going to spend the next five years defending him in court if he left the casino. Which one do you want?"

How he had planned to cover up this clusterfuck of a mess, Sal had no fucking idea, but he was grateful it wasn't going to be the Caruso's problem. He'd let Kent take the responsibility of cleaning up Valerie's sticky situation this one time, at least considering he was certain Justice had orchestrated the Caruso's involvement with Valerie in the first place.

"Is it possible for me to take the flash drive?" Sal's interest had been piqued about what kind of bug it must contain.

Kent's lips quirked into a smile at the endless possibilities The Great Salvatore might conduce with it in the future. "I don't care how justice gets carried out, only that justice is done."

Sal was grateful Valerie hadn't heard Kent say that line.

She was a few feet ahead, asking a man covered in facial scars that went by the name Jackal to model for her next video game.

Holding out a hand, he decided to let bygones be bygones. "Thank you, Kent."

"Don't thank me." The lawyer happily accepted the handshake. "You were the one who had the bright idea of splitting up just in case she got off on the tenth floor."

Shaking his head, Sal had to swallow his pride for what he was actually thanking him for. "Not that ..."

"Oh." Kent silently understood. "So, you no longer hate me for pushing you to buy that house next to Valerie?"

Hearing Valerie ask Jackal if he had scars anywhere else on his body had Sal giving the hand in his a death grip. "I wouldn't go that far just yet."

"I'm coming," Valerie huffed out to Sal, waving bye to her dozen new motorcycle friends while he dragged her along toward the ambulance.

"We really got to step up our game." Vincent also gave one last appreciative look back. Not at the men but their weapons.

"I'll get Lucca right on it," Sal hissed out, already planning on how he was going to use his new weapons to eradicate every good-looking man on Earth who came within a five-foot distance of Valerie.

As they crossed the street, Sal looked up at the blue moon one last time, grateful to still be alive.

"So, what's the deal with you and a blue moon?" Valerie asked curiously, noticing him staring at it.

"For fuck's sake ..." Vincent just shook his head and rolled his eyes heavenward at the superstition that Sal hadn't yet told her about.

"It's a long story."

MEN, GOD BLESS THEM. THEY WERE SO FULL OF THEMSELVES

Sitting cross-legged on the bed, she flipped through a computer magazine she had found in the bottom drawer of the nightstand while Sal took his shower. He had refused to let her take a shower with him after she almost knocked him unconscious while convincing him to try a new sexual position they hadn't done yet.

A while ago, when Valerie had first opened the drawer, she thought she had found his secret stash of porn. She'd heard all men had them. She'd decided to do some investigating in his room when she grew bored while he worked. Did Sal have any pictures or memorabilia from any of his former girlfriends he hadn't gotten rid of?

She planned to dispose of anything she considered came from a woman but hadn't found anything except for an old photo of a young boy with a woman standing in front of the exact kind of car Sal owned that Valerie swore she'd never eat Taco Bell in again after knowing the importance of the car and the fast food chain.

The child in the photo, she easily recognized as Sal. The beautiful woman, she immediately knew to be his mother, Isabella. His mother had a carefree yet wild allure about her that drew your eyes right to her. Valerie only wished she could have met her. She also couldn't help but notice the demons that haunted her hollow eyes that were reminiscent of the ones Sal carried today.

She pulled the picture closer to her chest before she placed it back where it belonged and started her search back up again. That was when she had found his stash ...

As she flipped through the hefty stack of computer magazines, she came to the conclusion they were porn for Sal. She, too, kinda got hot staring at a couple of the computers featured in the magazines.

Growing frustrated that Sal was taking so long, she was about to join him in the shower whether he wanted her to or not, but then the bathroom door opened. Valerie stretched her legs out as she eyed Sal's lean body. He looked like a tasty snack in only wearing a towel wrapped around his hips. Her eyes drifted to where he had tucked it in low at his waist, which happened to be right below the bullet hole scar he now carried.

"You know, I've been thinking." Valerie eyed the scar that only made him look that much tastier to her while her heart went all mushy whenever she thought about him saving her life that night. "We should discuss our future."

Sal wadded up the towel he had been using to roughly dry his hair and tossed it toward the laundry hamper that sat in the bathroom; he missed.

She tried not to laugh too hard at the failure, when Sal sheepishly went back to the bathroom to put the towel where it belonged.

He kept his apartment meticulously clean, *for reasons she now understood as well*. But, for some reason, he thought he was Michael Jordan when it came to his towels.

She had to kindly remind him more than once he never even played basketball growing up and still had yet to do so, as he continued only sitting behind a computer screen. It wasn't like she minded; athletes had never and would never be her thing.

"You want to talk about money or something?" he asked, trying to figure out where she was going with this.

Valerie rolled her eyes at him. "No, I don't want to talk about money."

"Good. Because I have enough money to buy you whatever you want. If Game Hookup isn't interested in your game after the changes you want to make, we'll be fine."

She had been hard at work on her game again, reworking some of the characters. She planned to resubmit it within the coming days, but she couldn't help herself not to get distracted from her point, as her interest in money perked up.

"You do?"

"Yep. Unless you want a mansion like Lucca's, then we will have to start smaller."

Her heart turned gooier. She had to selfishly admit she did like that he had money. After being broke her whole adult life and struggling from paycheck to paycheck, and then to no paycheck, it was nice to not have to worry about how she could afford groceries anymore. Especially when the groceries just showed up, thanks to Sal. Even if they were all pretty much organic. Plus, she could use some money for one of those computer parts she had been ogling in one of his magazines ...

She'd lost track of what she had wanted to talk about, when Sal's voice drew her out of her virtual world and back to the real one.

"Do you not like it here at the Casino Hotel? I thought you did."

Valerie sighed. "*Love*, Sal. I want to talk about *love*."

"You want to talk about love in general, or, like, you and me?" he stammered out.

Valerie gave him a warning look. She had stayed at his penthouse for almost a month now since they left the hospital after Sal got shot. Since then, they had yet to separate from each other unless Sal went to work.

She hadn't yet breached the topic of anything about them as a couple in the future because she had been waiting on three little words from him before she wanted to make plans of what her new future could look like. Valerie had known up on that rooftop, when she thought he had died, that she had officially fallen in love with him. She had cried so hard and gotten so scared because she thought she had lost the man of her dreams.

Sal hated the fact she continued to ask other men to be in her games, but Valerie no longer didn't want to put him in a video game because, like Sal, she was jealous and had no plans on sharing him with the rest of the world.

"Me *and* you." She made it clear that now was the time to rip off the Band-Aid to find out if he didn't have the same feelings she had for him. If Valerie didn't find out today, she was never going to recover from having to walk away from him. Sal could have easily changed his mind about making her his girlfriend over the past month, wishing he had just kept her as a fuck buddy. After living with her for that long, she supposed he could do that.

"Don't you think that if we are going to discuss money, we should talk about our feelings first?"

"Suuuure."

"You know, Sal, you're looking like less of a snack right

about now and more so like a piece of broccoli," she huffed out in frustration.

Sal could only stare at her in a stupor. "You're comparing me to food?"

Scooting to the bottom of the bed to where Sal was standing, she untucked his towel and let it drop to the floor. "I adore food." The words came out huskily. "Some, I *love.* Like snacks, for instance. Then some, I can leave and never touch them again."

"That's rather harsh," he commented, staring her down with lust in his enormously deep eyes. "Some foods just need to cook a bit longer before you can enjoy the full taste."

Her hand went to his joystick, running her thumb tenderly over the head. "I don't. I only need one taste to see if I like something."

Letting her hand slide down his cock, she covered the head with her mouth before she started sucking his cock fully into her mouth. Sal's thigh muscles started bulging as he got hot. She loved it when his made man façade transformed into a normal one who was never sure if he was going to get laid or not. His vulnerability that he was slowly showing her more every day made her want to make him happier, which in turned made her happier.

Clasping his dick tighter in her hand, she glided up and down on his cock smoothly while using her tongue to flick across his head when she reached the tip.

Sal ran his fingers through her hair before holding on. He was so gentle with her, as if afraid he might hurt her if he were to let himself go. Men, God bless them. They were so full of themselves.

His engorged cock got hotter and thicker, as if he were

going to climax at any second, but she wasn't going to let that happen just yet. She wanted to go along for the ride.

Removing him from her mouth, she let her lips travel to the inside of his thigh. "I love you, Sal," she said, placing a kiss on his sensitive skin. She felt the skin underneath her mouth jump, as if he was afraid. "Are you afraid I'm going to bite you?"

"N-No."

"You jumped when I told you I loved you."

"Okay, maybe I did think you were going to bite me," he admitted.

Standing, she turned them around until his back was to the bed and pushed him down. Then she watched the bed shake when he landed hard on the mattress.

Her hands moved up to her hips, then higher, and she slung her blue-black hair over her shoulder. "Salvatore Lastra, do you love me or not?"

"Oh, I love you," he promised, his eyes sliding down her form.

Satisfied with his answer ... for now, she launched herself at him, landing on his chest. "I'm going to show you how much I love you," she bragged then gave him a warning glare. "Then you can show me how much you love me."

Not taking it personally that Sal looked afraid, she went back to her favorite pastime activity. Gaming had been her number one for so long that she was still excited about the change in hobbies.

She lined her center up with his shaft, then lowered herself on top of him, moaning in ecstasy as she sank deeper. "You always feel so good."

"I haven't done anything yet."

"Your dick speaks for itself." She let him in on the secret that she bet any woman who had slept with him before had been desperate for seconds, but Valerie was prideful in being the only one. Taking all of him inside of her to the hilt, she lowered her heavy head onto his chest, and his arms surrounded her as he clasped her to him.

"You okay?" he asked, worry in his heady tone. "You stopped moving."

"I'm enjoying the moment."

Sal's chest started shaking underneath her cheek in a small laugh.

Unable to sit still long, she straightened to start moving on him again.

His beautiful eyes watched her as he twirled a strand of her hair around his finger, using the end of the strand to lightly tease her nipple.

"I love you, Valerie. You didn't have to ask me if I love you. It was plain to see if you'd just looked. I love that when you get scared, you act crazy. I love that we share the same love of computers. I *especially* love that you love sex," he groaned, bucking his hips under hers. He stopped his teasing to grab her hips in a tight grip, pulling her harder down on him. "You have a crazy-as-fuck sense of humor and do even crazier things without thinking them through. But you still frighten me, Valerie, and that's the truth."

She stopped riding him. "How do I still frighten you?"

Flipping her over without warning, he pressed into her beneath him until she felt surrounded by him. "Because I thought I might lose you up on that rooftop, and I don't know how I'm supposed to survive if anything ever happens to you."

"Nothing's going to happen to me."

"You can't promise that any more than me not dying during a blue moon." Sal's large hand cupped her cheek as his voice went so small from pain. "I'd die if I had to go back to being alone ... and I don't want to be alone again."

"You won't ever be alone," Valerie promised him while secretly promising to herself that Sal would never have to feel that pain again, not if she could help it. "You have too much family now," she softly reminded him of the blessing he had found.

Arching under Sal when he started moving again, she raised her legs to his hips, holding on tightly as Sal showed her just how much he loved her. And when she felt him climax inside of her, she let herself break apart in his arms, whispering in his ear how much she loved him, wanting to make up for all the times she had wanted to tell him over the past month.

She expected Sal to go to sleep after they had sex and was thinking about sneaking a snack. However, her eyes flew open when she felt herself lifted out of the bed.

"Why are you taking me to the bathroom? I was going to sleep."

Sal turned on the shower. "No, you weren't. You were waiting for me to fall asleep so you could get a MoonPie. You sleep a total of four hours, and you're done for the next twenty. All the sugar you're consuming keeps you from getting more sleep."

She didn't bother to tell The Great Salvatore that he was, in fact, wrong and that he didn't know everything about her yet.

Until she had turned eighteen and left home, every gram of sugar she had consumed had been monitored. Her stepmother had been a fanatic about it, believing the same thing Sal did—that sugar was the culprit of only needing a few hours of sleep and constantly being hyped up. It wasn't the sugar; it was simply how she was wired. She just didn't require a lot of sleep, and she was always hyped up because life was too short to miss out on what made you happy.

"So, you think a shower is going to help me sleep?" She wasn't against the shower; she would just rather have the snack. Not to mention two showers in one night was a bit excessive for him.

"No, I thought you might want to try that position we tried the last time that didn't work."

I can wait to eat …

"You think you'll be able to make me exhausted enough to sleep longer?"

Sal nodded slyly, like a fox. "Yes."

Taking off her favorite oversized T-shirt she had stolen from Sal, she opened the shower door. "I'm always ready to play, baby. Just don't blame me when you're lagging."

EVERY DAY AFTER

"I can't live like this, Sal!" Valerie slammed the pantry cabinet with a thud. While she was grateful her dream came true of Sal bringing in the groceries, he was stingy when it came to buying her candy and sweets, trying to help her with her addiction.

"I just bought those yesterday." He nodded toward the empty box of MoonPies on the counter.

"Well, you had a few yourself," she muttered in frustration.

Sal quickly corrected her. "Yeah. Two."

She was about to burst into tears, when Sal wrapped his arms around her in a tight embrace. She had been waiting on pins and needles for a phone call for the last week, and her cravings were at an all-time high.

"You're just stressed out, baby. Would you like me to fuck you again?"

"No—I mean, I do," she quickly explained, trying to relax in his warm arms. "It's just that it's only been five minutes since the last time we did it, and then ten minutes before that. The last time we did it back-to-back like that, you wouldn't let me touch you for two days."

"Yeah, that might not be the best idea, then," he agreed, remembering. You could tell even Sal couldn't believe the predicament he had landed himself in by unlocking a secret nymphomaniac.

Placing a tender kiss on her forehead, he began to drag her out of the penthouse. "Come on; I think I might have something else to take your mind off it."

"What is it?" she asked eagerly, strolling along beside him, hand in hand. She'd do just about anything to forget that she had resubmitted her game to Game Hookup with her updated characters.

"I think I found a new job for you to do here at the Casino Hotel in the meantime."

Valerie almost couldn't believe the suggestion; she'd tried and failed at multiple different jobs already. Sal couldn't even find her a computer job underneath him, as she had almost driven him crazy. "Are you sure?"

"Yeah, I think this time, I finally found the perfect job for you. There's absolutely *no way* you could fuck this one up."

Yeah, right! Not even Valerie's own mind was so sure. All she knew was that Sal was on a time crunch to find her a job that would keep her busy enough so he could spend time working for Lucca and less time fucking her.

Taking her to the elevator, Sal hit a series of buttons to take them to the casino without stopping. When the doors closed them inside, he pulled her in for a gentle kiss.

Valerie adored his kisses. Actually, she adored absolutely everything about him. He was sweet and kind, just like she had told Justic—*erm* Kent—those words were the best way to describe Sal once she got to know him. While she herself verged on sour and deranged.

Before him, she had lived inside video games; he, himself, inside a computer. But when they left those worlds and entered their own reality that they were beginning to create together, it was no longer like the oil and water mixture they had at the start. It had become that sweet spot where the moon met the ocean.

Parting her lips for his tongue to enter, she captured it appreciatively, turning his gentle kiss wild, much like she always did. When the elevator opened, he groaned before wrapping an arm around her shoulders.

Valerie couldn't help but smile to herself. It was just another thing she had come to adore about him. Sal loved showing the world that she was his, and while he did his best to keep his jealousy in check, she didn't mind being reminded of the fact that she had fallen in love with a protective made man. She especially loved it when it was The Great Salvatore who used his talent for her protection.

What can I say? Valerie couldn't help it; she was weak for a man who wore glasses and sat behind a computer screen.

Besides, he had absolutely nothing to worry about. She would never want another man. Even the men she'd put in her video games were only for inspiration, as not a one could rival the diamond she had secured.

Plus ... Maria was already taken.

"Did you ever decide what you want to do with our houses on Prairie Drive?" he asked, beginning to lead her through the busy casino after exiting the elevator. "We could always just topple them both and build one large home?"

"And show our faces in that neighborhood again?" Valerie scoffed at the thought. "Hell no. You burned the last bridge by stealing Katie's car."

Okay, so, Sal didn't end up being Mister fucking Rogers, but it definitely wasn't his fault why they couldn't live there anymore. The bridge had been first dosed in gasoline the night her ass had gotten arrested and she acted like she belonged in the looney bin. Even with the charges against Valerie being officially dropped, and the real cyber attacker being revealed, the "figurative" bridge had actually burned to a crisp the day they got into a fight. Her excessive honking down Prairie Drive as she flicked him off had every neighbor coming outside to join him. And an awestruck Katie, who had spread the word that Sal had stolen her car, might not have done them any favors in being able to return, but—

"Yeah, you're probably right," he finally agreed, giving in to that fact. It was always better to just agree with Valerie on certain things that didn't matter much anyway. It was actually something he was beginning to learn rather quickly. "You want me to sell them, then?"

"Sure, if you can get someone to buy my shit hole of a fire hazard house, that'd be great!"

That, Sal didn't doubt. His home had been more or less the same in the wiring department. Thankfully, he had bought it to unplug himself from the outside world and had no intentions of looking at a computer screen there after sitting in front of one at work all day.

"I might know some people interested ..." He laughed at the thought. Their new neighbors on both sides of the penthouse were beginning to loathe them.

Sal had absolutely no problem showing off who he was with behind closed doors now. He had gone from the least laid made man to the most overnight, and every occupant on the top floor knew it. They also had no plans to move out of the Casino Hotel anytime soon. They were both perfectly content where they were in life, as each one of them was dedicated to their passions and work. They also enjoyed the close proximity to his demanding job being right down the hall. Not to mention, Valerie was beginning to enjoy the perks of living here as well. She could visit him for a quickie anytime she wanted, and there were endless amounts of electricity and working outlets. To top it all off, he was about to reveal possibly the biggest perk of all.

"Here we are," Sal said, showing her his last hope of finding her a job at the Casino Hotel.

As she stared up at the sign, Valerie's mouth dropped open. "How did I not realize the Casino Hotel had a gift shop?"

"Must've forgotten to mention it, I guess." That definitely wasn't true. Sal had always been sure to even take them the long way *around* it.

With her going inside and heading straight for the candy section, Sal couldn't believe he didn't think of this sooner. This was the absolute perfect job for Valerie. Her working here meant he no longer had to personally fund her snacking and sugar addiction; he could make Lucca pay for it through the Casino Hotel. If Lucca wanted Valerie to have a job so badly after putting Chloe in her video game, then he was going to get it.

Hell, Lucca wanted him to get back to work, right? He had barely gotten a thing done that didn't involve screwing, and this was the only option left that would not only make his boss happy but meant his pant size could return to normal. Keeping snacks and candy in his place was starting to come at a severe cost to more than just his wallet. Valerie had an endless metabolism as one of her superpowers. He, however, did not.

Giving a wave to the kind young girl behind the cash register who had only just started working here herself, he began to worry a bit. "Winnie here is going to teach you everything you need to know. Do you think you'll be okay?"

"Are you kidding? This is heaven!" she squealed with delight, going up to her toes to place a kiss on his lips after already cracking open a bag of Twizzlers. "Thank you."

"Yeah, don't thank me yet," he muttered under his breath, glad he had already given Winnie his contact number in case this went south. "Let's see how today goes."

"But you said so yourself; there's absolutely *no way* I could fuck this one up."

"Right," he said, giving her goodbye kiss on the lips. "I'm going to my office to try to get a few things done."

"Okay. Love ya! Bye!" she said, not worried in the slightest, already inspecting what her new workplace had to offer in inventory.

Leaving her there, he threw up a quick prayer to God that she'd at least last a few hours, which might give him enough time for what he needed to take care of.

"THANK YOU. COME AGAIN."

Valerie looked up from the magazine she was flipping through as Winnie handed the customer her bag with the kindest smile. "Nice customer," she praised as the customer happily walked away. "I think I'm getting the hang of it. I just need to watch you ring up *four or five* more customers, and I think I'll have it."

That wasn't true. Valerie had gotten it from the first go around, but it'd be harder to enjoy her magazine and endless Twizzlers once Winnie realized she did.

The girl scratched her head in slight confusion. "How did you convince Sal to let work at the gift shop again?"

Pulling out another Twizzlers, Valerie felt Winnie's eyes on her. "I think he wanted to get rid of me so he could get some work done for a few hours."

Moving in front of the counter, Winnie started restocking the candy. Valerie dipped her head back to the magazine at the girl's accusatory glance.

"Who does Sal work with here at the Casino Hotel?"

Valerie raised her eyes at the weird tone in Winnie's voice then tried to hide a knowing smile once she might have realized the source of the question. It didn't hurt to confirm her thoughts. "Why are you wondering?"

"I'm just curious …" Winnie tried giving an indifferent shrug that Valerie saw right through before coming back behind the counter to sit down on the stool next to hers. Opening a bag of Starbursts for herself, Valerie's eyes dropped to the red Starburst in her hand as she started peeling the wrapper. "I'm stuck in here all the time, and I'm not allowed on the casino floor. I don't know much about anything about anyone who works here or what their jobs are."

"Join the club," Valerie huffed out. Sal didn't want her meeting any of the men who worked here. While she was allowed on the casino floor, she figured Winnie wasn't because the girl didn't look to be twenty-one yet. The sweet girl was lucky to be eighteen, by the looks of it. Her flame-orange hair, chubby red cheeks, and freckles really solidified

Winnie's fate of having to be carded until she at least reached thirty years of age.

Watching Winnie choose her next Starburst that matched her flame-colored hair, Valerie's mouth watered. Everyone knew orange was the best.

"Can I have one?"

Winnie held out her hand with the Starburst in it. "Sure."

"I know what some of the guys do," she politely offered after snatching the candy with lightning-fast reflexes to pop it into her mouth. "Others, I don't."

Carefully taking out another orange Starburst, Winnie slowly unwrapped the candy with painstaking precision. "I didn't say I wanted to know about *a guy* that works here, per se ..."

"Please." Valerie eyed her and the piece of candy. She knew when a girl wanted info on a guy, and this was definitely it. "Now, who is it you are curious about?" Valerie asked before Winnie could place the candy in her mouth.

Slumping her shoulders, the girl finally gave in, "Amo."

Valerie happily snatched the candy cube. Amo, she definitely had gotten acquainted with. "What would you like to know?"

Winnie sat up straight, losing all pretenses. "What job does he do in the casino?"

She had to think for a moment of what she could tell the girl. "Well, he works on the very bottom floor of the casino."

"But this is the bottom floor?"

At her confusion, Valerie simply played dumb. "Is it?"

Getting serious, Winnie took out another Starburst before rephrasing her question. It was obvious she knew something shady went on in the Casino Hotel, but she had yet to know what that was. "What's Amo's job?"

Yellow. Everyone knew yellow was the worst. "You have any more orange?"

Winnie switched the yellow out for the orange.

"Security guard." Valerie couldn't help it; she was easy.

"Really?"

"Yup," she confirmed, popping the orange square in her mouth without remorse for being bought so easily. "You should see him walking around, checking on all the dealers and making sure everything is on the up and up from time to time."

Winnie leaned to the side in her chair, trying to take a peek out the giftshop door to look out onto the casino floor. "How come I've never seen him?"

"Must be missing him." Valerie shrugged.

"Interesting." The girl mulled it over before giving up in trying to find him when she almost fell sideways out of her chair. "That makes sense, considering how b—" Her cheeks grew a brighter red after realizing she had gotten a bit too comfortable speaking. "*Big* he is."

It was hard for Valerie not to chuckle a bit when Winnie forced the last bit of her sentence out, but she didn't, not wanting to embarrass the sweet young girl.

Seeing her peel the yellow Starburst, Valerie generously didn't take it from her but eyed the rest of the bag. She thought about getting up and taking a new bag for herself, but one glance at the trash can, she stopped herself. She already owed a huge tab on what she'd already eaten, and she had been wanting that bag of Skittles.

"Does he have a girlfriend?" the girl sheepishly mumbled.

It was a question Valerie had to ask many times herself about Sal. Smiling to herself, she didn't blame the girl, having been in the same predicament herself just a short time ago. But knowledge came at a price ... "You got more orange Starbursts?"

Digging in the bag, Winnie held out five.

Damn, she liked this girl.

"You have a serious sugar addition," Winnie told her with slight concern on her face.

"Tell me about it." Taking the candy away, Valerie started peeling the wrappers. "What I really want is my vape. Candy replaces the urge."

"You could replace the urge with healthy alternatives, like celery or carrot sticks," Winnie offered helpfully.

"I'm using a three-step process to quit. I'm using candy to get over the urge to vape, then when I have that beat, I'll switch to healthy alternatives."

Winnie watched her open the last Starburst curiously. "How long has it been since you stopped vaping?"

"*A while* ..." she finally choked out, too embarrassed to put a number on it.

"I think I'd ditch the three-step process. You're stuck on step two."

"You're right. I need to give serious thought about what my next step should be," Valerie agreed with her newfound friend, swallowing. "You got any more red ones?"

Winnie held out the bag. "Here; you can have the bag."

Smiling, she wiggled her brows at her. "Since you're being so generous, I'll ask around about Amo just for you."

Suddenly, the bag was snatched right back out of her hands. "Don't. I was just being curious. If you ask, then they could assume I like him. I'd *die* if that happens."

"I don't think you'd die ..." Valerie retorted when a broad-shouldered man came through the doors.

Jumping off the stool, she shimmied up to the cash register, giving Winnie a wink. "I got you, girl."

"Valerie, please don't embarrass me!" Winnie hissed from beside her, trying to shove her out of the way.

Elbowing her back, Valerie shot her a warning glance, pointing at the stool. "Sit."

Pivoting back, she saw Amo coming to the counter and played it cool. "How's it going, Amo?"

"Good."

Valerie started ringing up the pack of gum, chips, and two Gatorades, like she had done it a million times before. Welp, there went trying to get out of ringing up the next five customers. "Feeling dehydrated?"

Amo didn't break a smile at her friendly chatter, and he didn't answer her question either. So, she decided to try a different tactic after looking over secretly at Winnie.

"Sal and I are planning on going to a movie this weekend. If you have a girlfriend, we could do a double date. It's more fun to go with another couple."

Amo held out his credit card to tap it on the machine. "What's the movie?"

Valerie had to quickly think what was out and what the big oaf would want to see, as well. "*Mission Impossible*."

"What night are you wanting to go?"

Why couldn't he just answer the fucking question with a yes or no? Now she had to think of the best night that he would actually want to go. Friday and Saturday would be busy, and Amo would have to work, so would Sal. "Sunday."

"I have to work Sunda—"

"We could go another night," she quickly offered before rambling on. "I'll ask Sal what other night would be good for him. So, are you up for a double date? Do you need to check with your girlfriend what night she's available?"

"You're better off asking someone else," Amo told her

unhelpfully. "Nero and Vincent are scheduled for the day shifts. Elle or Lake love going to the movies, but I don't see them wanting to see *Mission Impossible*."

"Exactly why I didn't ask them ..." she mumbled, feeling just as defeated as poor Winnie looked.

"You could ask—"

"Never mind," Valerie cut him off, giving up on her own mission impossible. Amo was helpless. "I'll leave it up to Sal. He can figure it out. Have a nice day."

Grabbing his drinks and his other purchases, Amo left them staring after him.

Valerie turned back to Winnie. "Are you sure you like him? I think he's a dick." How the man couldn't see Winnie was in love with him by a single look defied her imagination. *Boys, they're so oblivious.*

"I didn't say I *liked* him." Turning bright red, Winnie started putting out some keychains. "Only that I was *curious* about him."

"You know the first thing that attracted me to Sal?"

The girl looked back at her. "No, what?"

"How hot he was," she confided. "Of course, I had to get past the strong and silent part of his personality."

"Amo is hot." Red seeped down from her cheeks to her chest as her head hung low. "Too bad he doesn't even know I'm alive."

"You know that isn't true," she tried consoling the lovesick girl. "It's not like he thinks a robot is ringing him up when he comes in here."

"I might as well be a robot—a *fat* robot." Glumly, she picked up one of the keychains to play with. "He probably has a lot of women he goes out with that are prettier than me."

"You're very pretty." Valerie stared her down intently to

make sure the girl understood that. Life was already hard for a girl in this cruel world; adding societal pressures on women of needing to fit inside a box of what was pretty by societies pressures didn't help. She knew that better than anyone, considering how she dressed. However, men were dumb dogs, and Valerie didn't want to get her hopes to high.

She didn't know anything about Amo's personal life. He could have a steady girlfriend, and it wouldn't be fair to raise Winnie's hopes up if there was no chance of getting with him. It was obvious her confidence was already a bit low by the way Winnie talked about herself.

"Besides looks shouldn't matter, anyway."

"Didn't you say Sal's looks was the first thing you noticed about him?"

"I admit, I'm a shallow person," she said, putting a hand over her chest before scooping all the empty wrappers in the now empty bag and throwing it into the full trash can. "It's okay for women to be shallow—it's endearing. When men do it, they're womanizing assholes. Just from the little I've been around Amo, he doesn't come across as *that much* of a womanizer." She couldn't say the same about the asshole part ...

"I don't think so either," Winnie agreed helplessly. "He seems too sad to be a womanizer."

Damn. The girl had it bad. Amo didn't come across as sad. He came across as if he carried a big chip on already massive shoulders. The few times she had been around him, after Sal had made it clear she was taken, he'd sported a grouchy face and had the personality of an eighty-year old, crotchety old man.

"You don't think he figured out why you mentioned a girlfriend, do you?" Winnie asked, taking the pack of Skittles from her before she could open it.

Valerie snatched the candy right back before ripping open the package without remorse, knowing Sal could pay the tab. This love stuff was just taxing on her soul. "Of course not. How could he? I was smooth as silk."

HE WAS BEGINNING TO THINK HIS PRAYER WAS working, but then his phone lit up with a call from Winnie.

Fuck. He answered it only to say that he'd be right there. He'd wait until he was there to find out what she had done in person.

He made his own call on the way to the gift shop, as he had officially given up trying to work until Valerie sold her game. Once she did, she'd begin working on her new game, and then his life could go back to somewhat normalcy.

"I haven't heard from you in a bit. How ya been, kid?" His old friend's voice came over the line.

"Pretty good, but it sounds like you're doing better than me these days."

The happiness and carefree attitude was easily notice-able through the phone, along with the sound of the ocean.

"Oh, definitely," his friend quickly assured him that he was currently living the life. "Cabo is great this time of year. You and Valerie should come take a trip down here."

"Maybe soon." At this rate, he'd be in Cabo tomorrow, and jobless. Clearing his throat, Sal prepared himself to ask his request and the reason for the phone call. "Listen, I'm wondering if you have anything on the company Game Hookup? For some reason, they're dragging their feet on offering Valerie a deal. So, I'd like you to hurry them up, if it's possible for you to do that from where you currently are."

"Sure, I could do that for you, kid, but can't you do that yourself?" He laughed, knowing Sal's secret firsthand of being The Great Salvatore.

"Yes, but I don't want Valerie ever finding out I might have *persuaded* them into giving her a deal." She possessed the same skills he did, and there was no hiding anything from Valkyrie these days. "We both know her game is better than anything they've brought to market in recent years, anyway. I'm just hurrying them up to the inevitable."

"Ah, I understand. I'm sure I'll have Bubblegum Blitz bought by the end of the day."

Sal smiled, positive that would be the case. He had learned from the best, after all. "Thank you, Terry."

"No problem, Sal. Take care of yourself."

"You, too," Sal told him before ending the call, positive he would do exactly that.

Terry was living better than anyone in the world; Sal always saw to that. Giving the world to the man who had brought Dante Caruso to him was one of his greatest accomplishments in life. If it weren't for Terry being brave enough to ever call Dante in the first place, knowing it could have cost him his life if Lucifer had ever found out, Sal's life wouldn't be what it was today. Hiding behind a screen could only take you so far in life; you had to also live it.

When he made it to the gift shop, Sal didn't even have to ask, because he already saw the devastation. The only thing that was shocking was that Dante was there at the door, waiting for him.

"Sal, I'm not sure why you thought having her work here would ever be a good idea. She'll fucking eat us out of business."

"I'm not sure, either," he agreed in defeat, seeing the full trash can of empty bags. "I'm sorry."

"She might need to see a doctor." Dante looked back at her for confirmation that she was still eating. "Or a psychiatrist."

Sal had to admit she might have a small problem if Dante Caruso was telling her to see a shrink.

"Nadia has a few she works with for her charity; would you like her to send you some numbers?"

"That's okay." He waved him off, knowing all their problems would soon be solved. "So, what are you doing here?"

"Well, I was coming up to smoke a cigar in Lucca's office"—with the story starting off with his own vice, Dante's recommendation of seeking help sounded a bit less compelling—"when I decided to come check on Winnie. She's been a part of Nadia's youth outreach for a while, so I was just seeing how she was doing when I walked into *this*."

Sal had to admit that the barren walls Dante motioned toward did help put his case back on track.

"The poor girl tried to hold off on calling you, thinking Valerie would eventually stop eating the inventory, but I told Winnie that if she didn't get your ass down here soon, she might start chewing through the walls next."

"You can have her send the numbers," Sal finally agreed.

"I think that might be wise, son." Dante nodded before softening his voice from his stern one. "Love her, though, truly, but *wise*."

He couldn't help but notice his father figure had softened not only with time but with Nadia's love. In fact, all the Caruso men had softened from their woman's love, and Sal was no different.

In that moment, Sal couldn't help himself as he brought Dante in for a hug.

"You okay?" Dante asked, surprised by the action.

"Yes," he assured him with a laugh, and his eyes went misty. "I just never thanked you for the day you picked me up when my mother died."

Dante wrapped his arms tightly around his son with his own tears forming in his icy gaze. "You never had to."

"I know," Sal told him, believing it. Dante had never asked him anything in return for his kindness. Anything Sal did for him, including joining the family, had been of his own mind. "But thank you. Thank you for that day and every day after. I'll never be able to repay you for the wonderful life you have given me."

"And you'll never have to," Dante promised him. "Love you, son."

Sal finally said the word he had never been able to say before. "Love you, too, *Dad*."

SAL WAS WATCHING VALERIE SLOWLY UNDRESS WHEN his phone vibrated against his chest. Accepting the call, his eyes didn't waiver from his girl's assets. "I'm kind of busy."

"This won't take a second." Amo's voice came over the line. "I want you to put a stop to Valerie's matchmaking."

"**I** have a very addictive personality."

You don't say? he thought; better to not speak the fucking obvious out loud.

"It's not fair that you don't have an addiction," she continued pitifully as she was dragged out of the gift shop. "You wouldn't get it."

Sal threw her his own look of pity. "Who says I don't?"

"Yeah, right," she huffed, giving up and letting him lead her away. "The only thing you're addicted to is buying organic snacks."

"Because I used to eat out of a dumpster," he reminded her calmly.

"Oh, right." At the reminder that it could always be worse, her mood lightened. "Fuck Game Hookup. I'll start my own company if I have to."

"That's okay. I have a feeling they'll be calling you soon."

"You think?" Valerie asked hopefully while also chewing on her nails nervously. It was another habit she was starting up while waiting for an answer from the company.

"They'll have no other option but to," he promised nonchalantly. "Just give it till the end of the day. If they don't by then, I'll be the first to invest in your new company. Then I'll make Lucca your second."

"Okay," Valerie said gleefully, knowing it was a win-win either way. "What should we do in the meantime?"

Sal brought her closer to his body in a sudden rush. While he was at work, he had gotten a notification that a movie-accurate Harlequin cosplay costume that went with her bat had arrived. He had to go back to receiving all his mail here at the Casino Hotel, but it wasn't that big of a deal to swing by the front desk to get it. As long as it didn't have a picture on it of what was inside the box.

You win some, you lose some.

Leaning down, he hovered his lips a few centimeters above hers in a sensual smile. "I have a few ideas that come to mind."

VALERIE ENTERED THE UNDERGROUND FOR THE second time, but this time, she did so alone as she sat at the barren Black Jack table, just like she had been told.

"Sorry, honey, this table is currently closed." The female pit boss came over, giving her an apologetic smile and waving to a table that was already almost full. "At this time of day, we're a bit slow, but you can join this table over here."

"Oh, I'm so sorry!" Valerie quickly explained, "It's just my first time playing, and I'm a bit nervous to join another table, but I totally underst—"

"That's okay, sweetie; you can stay right there." The pit boss kept her from getting up to join the group of men after seeing the apprehension on her face. "I always love a good reason to deal again, so what the hell? I'll help you out."

Relieved, Valerie puffed out a huff of air. "My gosh, thank you so much. That is so kind of you!"

"Of course. It will be my pleasure to show you the ropes. What's your name, honey?"

The gorgeous woman with blonde streaks through her hair looked like she belonged on the front of a *Playboy* magazine. Getting an eyeful of her ginormous tits, Valerie adjusted the extravagant earrings that Sal had given her as a gift, already devising a plan to use them in his death if he wasn't able to talk his way out of this one the next time she heard his voice in person.

She racked her brain if Sal had taken this woman back to his house but definitely didn't remember her, and there was no fucking possible way you could ever forget a woman like the one who stood in front of her.

Ha-ha! He wishes!

"My name's Valerie. Yours?" she said, laying the light stack of cash down.

"Sadie." She took the cash and quickly turned the bills into chips. "It's nice to meet ya. I haven't seen a fresh face down here in a while, and it's always good to see such a pretty one."

"Aw, thanks. It's nice to meet you, too." Blushing, she took it more as a compliment from Sadie than she had with Amo as she watched her shuffle the deck with expert precision. While she did so, Sadie gave her a rundown of how to play the game and the rules.

"Think you're ready?"

"Yep. I think so ..." Valerie nodded as she began to deal

the cards. It started off as a no-brainer for Sadie to explain what she should do by the book of basic strategy when Valerie was dealt a twenty and the house revealing a face card.

Waving her hand above the table, Valerie was trying to stand. "Like this?"

"You got it!" Sadie praised as she flipped the house card to reveal a six and then busted on an eight. "See? You'll be a pro in no time."

Giving Sadie a wink, she ignored the small laughter in her ear. "Well, I'll have you to thank for that."

While the hands went on, they got trickier, but Valerie stopped to listen to her coach, sure to take her time in making the right call when it *came* to her. The hardest part was making sure no one wanted to sit down at the table with her and ruin her flow. She had to do everything she could to think of as a way to scare off the men, including letting them know that it was her time of the month and she might not make rational decisions at the moment.

While she talked with Sadie about her current blood flow, the last gentleman to sit next to her hadn't even set the chips down on the table before he scrammed.

"Wow. You're doing quite well," Sadie told her appreciatively as the chips began to fill the table. The pit boss totally caught on to what Valerie was doing by talking about her period but didn't seem to mind, enjoying the solo female company.

"Beginner's luck," she told her simply before moving on. "I'll have to put you into my next video game. You'd make for a sick character design."

Having heard all about her video game obsession, as she had now been sitting here for over an hour, Sadie's hand fell across her cleavage. "I'd be honored. What's this one about?"

"I think this time, I'm going to do more of a story campaign. Think *Law and Order* meets *The Godfather* meets *Sons of Anarchy*."

"Sounds interesting." Sadie smirked right before the house busted yet again.

When she dealt the next hand, Valerie had given her the sign to split.

"Are you sure you want to do that? The book doesn't recommen—"

"Oh, I'm sure." Valerie smiled sweetly.

Sadie split her tens, then dealt two tens to place on top of each hand, giving Valerie two hands of twenty. Doing this made the house bust as small cards flowed out next. However, the house wouldn't have busted if it had drawn that first ten.

Giving her her winnings, the pit boss couldn't believe the sheer luck. "Wow, that was something you just pulled off."

"Beginner's luck," Valerie told her again with a shrug, about to change the subject she had been saved, when Amo appeared behind Sadie.

"Hey, Sadie, I keep getting complaints that there's a woman asking men if they have any tampons or a pa—"

Neither Valerie nor Sadie could keep themselves from laughing, causing Amo to finally see who customers had been complaining about.

"I should have known," he said, shaking his head at her. "You've been the bane of my existence since you moved in with S—"

"We'll keep it down from now on," Valerie choked out, stopping him before he could finish his sentence and not only completely embarrass her but ruin the fun by mentioning who it was she had moved in with upstairs. Amo was her new next-door neighbor who hated her with a passion; this time, it was so much sweeter with a view and a boyfriend. "I promise."

"Okay, fine," Amo conceded, understanding what she was doing, but he had to still put his foot down or Lucca would kick his ass. "You can play for another hour by yourself at this table, but that's it."

"Aw, thanks, Amo." Valerie smiled at him but wished it had been less of one at his next words.

"You know, I could be a model for your game, too," he suggested with a hell of a lot of confidence. "Matthias isn't the only one around here with tattoos."

While that was news to her, considering she didn't think the Carusos were allowed them, she was still happy to burst his bubble. "Bubblegum Blitz has already been fully approved by Game Hookup. They're going to announce the release date soon," Valerie said with pride but then had to avert her eyes down to the table. "Maybe in the next, *next* one."

Both Sadie and Valerie burst out into tearful laughter at the inside joke that he wasn't even going to make it into her mafia video game.

Amo couldn't help himself from getting one last dig in before he left. "Just keep the fucking noises to a minimum the next time you two go at it."

She watched him walk away in shock from what he had said, but it took only a few seconds before both girls turned back into laughing hyenas.

"Hey, ladies." A cold voice had sat down beside Valerie, announcing his arrival and silencing their laughter. "What joke did I miss that sent Amo away like that?"

Seeing Lucca sitting right next to her had Valerie's heart pumping.

"Oh, nothing, just a little girl humor," Sadie told him while winking at Valerie.

Lucca, dressed in his all-black suit, took his Zippo and cigarettes from his front pocket and lit one up. "It seems you have collected quite the winnings, Valerie."

"Mmhmm." She nodded nervously, adjusting her hair over her earring.

"I didn't know you gambled," he said, expertly blowing a cloud of smoke in her direction. "I didn't even know you played."

"First time," she squeaked out after inhaling the intoxicating scent. The slight rush of nicotine made her heart rate calm enough to say her usual go-to. "Beginner's luck, I guess."

"That's some beginner's luck," he agreed, taking in the stash carefully to count how much she had accumulated.

Her hand drifted a little bit closer to his cigarettes. "Are you going to play or ...?"

"Let's see ..." He mulled the thought over before looking at Sadie. "How much did she put in?"

Sadie quickly ratted her out. "Five hundred."

Lucca picked up five hundred dollars' worth of her chips and took them for himself, putting them in the designated circle on the table all in one hand. It was a measly little stack in comparison to the amount she had accumulated. "I guess I will."

"Goddammit! Abort mission! Abort mission!"

The yelling voice that rang in her ear blasted beyond its usual capabilities as the earring was then snatched from her ear by Lucca and squashed like a bug into tiny little pieces in his hand.

Her huge, wide eyes had grown so much in fear at witnessing him obliterating her hidden earpiece, she began blurting out her words like vomit.

"I'm sorry! Sal made me do it! I didn't actually think he could really count the card—"

"It's all right, Valerie. You can relax," Lucca told her as he motioned for one of the servers to bring him two Jack and Cokes. "Sadie, do me a favor and go find where Amo went to. I think it's his turn to try his hand at dealing."

Valerie tried her best to take his advice and relax, but it was much easier when the drink arrived, followed by an upset Amo taking Sadie's place on the other side of the table. Not a peep came out of his mouth, taking his punishment of not realizing their scheme.

Satisfied with his demands, Lucca opened his pack of cigarettes and held one out in offering to Valerie. "Now, do *you really* want to play?"

Blinking in disbelief, she wondered if she was actually sleeping and merely just dreaming this impossible-to-believe scenario in her mind.

Fuck it. She accepted his offering; she would go back to her Twizzlers tomorrow. This was a once-in-a-lifetime experience, regardless of real or not real, and she was going to pick the brain of one of the most notorious mob bosses until he grew sick of her voice, and then she'd ask him permission to use it in her next game.

"Oh, and, Valerie." The Boogieman gave her a sinister smile and flipped the end of his antique Zippo that was engraved with the name Caruso. "Welcome to the family."

EPILOGUE

HAPPY BIRTHDAY

"I want to go out to eat tonight."

Sal looked away from the security footage he was watching to see Valerie nonchalantly sitting next to him. "I'm working."

Like always, Valerie didn't seem to mind that he was, but she kinda had a massive point, today of all days. "Who the hell works on their birthday? Ask someone else to work for you."

His gaze solemnly went back to the screens. "I told you I didn't want to celebrate my birthday."

"Who said we're going to celebrate your birthday?" she asked, waving that thought off. "I just want to go out to eat. Don't you get sick of eating here all the time?"

"No."

"Well, I do." An exasperated Valerie continued, "Come on; you can just watch me eat if you're not hungry."

Stern eyes drifted back to her. "We're not eating at Taco Bell."

Giving him one of those pitiful looks she had learned to

give to get her way, she knew she had won the battle before he did. "If I let you pick, can we go out?"

Was he ever going to tell this woman no?

"Let me see what I can do." At least that stopped her from pestering him for five minutes.

"I'll go get dressed." Hopping off the chair, no longer pouting, she gave him a kiss that had him pulling her down on his lap. "I thought you wanted me to leave."

"I do. I'm trying to work, and you're very distracting." Sal ran his hand under her oversized grumpy cat T-shirt to cup her breast.

Valerie grinned at him unrepentantly. "You take life too seriously."

When she started unbuttoning his shirt, he meant to stop her, but kisses always managed to destroy his good intentions. Pressing a button to electronically lock the door, he settled her more comfortable over his dick. "I take life seriously every time I make love to you, sweetheart."

"Aw ..." she cooed lovingly. "I love it when you talk sweet to me."

He also loved the fact she didn't wear a bra under her baggy shirts. Since she had started working on her new game, she didn't come to his office to hang out as much as she used to do. At first, he enjoyed the break from her constant presence. That lasted a whole hour. After his shift, he would go to their apartment, and she would make up for her absence. Squealing with happiness, she would barrel into him before he could practically shut the door.

An hour later, they would order something from one of the restaurants in the casino, and then she would show him what she had worked on that day. They would spend the rest of the evening watching old movies in bed before making love again then going to sleep in each other's arms.

His life had gone from spending most of his life alone to being loved unconditionally again.

Tilting Valerie's chin up, he stared into her eyes. "I don't think I could stand being alone again."

"You won't have to be," she promised him. "You're missing your mom today, aren't you?"

"Yes," he softly admitted. Hiding anything from Valerie was becoming nearly impossible. He had come to find out she was a much better hacker than himself.

"That's why you don't want to celebrate your birthday?" she asked, fiddling with a button on his shirt.

"She always made a big deal of my birthday." Sal dryly swallowed the lump in his throat at a memory, "One time, she'd manage to rake enough cash so we could stay at a hotel that day. We checked in while they still had the complimentary breakfast. It was the only time we didn't have to share a meal. We had eaten until we were full, and then went swimming in the pool till the sun went down. That was the only day we could pretend to be a normal family. For dinner, Mom had gone to Little Caesars for a five-dollar pizza, then we sat and watched TV until we fell asleep. In the morning, Mom had woken me up to eat again before we left. When we checked out of the hotel, we didn't know when we'd have another meal, but it didn't matter.

"Mom had her problems, but she taught me a very valuable lesson. You can survive anything, if you're with someone you love."

Valerie gave him a soft kiss on his cheek. "I'm sorry you're missing your mom, baby."

Before he could stop her, she had already shimmied out of his arms.

"I'm going to get dressed, and you're going to find

someone to fill your shift tonight," she said defiantly before clapping her hands together. "Now, hurry up!"

Pressing the button, he let her leave. Talking about his mom had brought out a sense of melancholy he had trouble shaking off. That was when he realized sitting in his office wasn't helping to relieve the aching void of her being gone. He then called Lucca, asking him to send someone to replace him for the rest of his shift.

Less than thirty minutes later, Amo showed up. Expecting Amo to give him a hard time, Sal was shocked when Amo took his vacated chair without mouthing off.

"You're not going to bust my chops because you had to come in?"

"I wasn't doing anything anyway. Besides, it's your birthday. Go enjoy your night off."

Taking a long look at Amo, Sal realized the man who was sitting in the chair was no longer a kid. He couldn't pinpoint when it had happened, but Sal could see a maturity in Amo, and he could no longer see an adolesecent trying to navigate his way into the adult world.

"Thanks, Amo," he said before leaving his office and heading to his penthouse.

Valerie was coming down the steps right when he came in the door.

"You're here!" As he walked toward her, Valerie launched herself into his arms. "I thought I was going to have go back to your office and drag you out of there."

"Amo took over for me." Giving her a quick kiss, he set her back down and looked her over appreciatively. Valerie had changed out of her comfortable pants and T-shirt to a pink, pleated plaid mini skirt, black tights, and boots, with a matching black blouse that had a pink frilly lace around the neckline that matched her skirt. "You look hot. You sure you want to go out." Sal's hand itched to pull that skirt up and play with what was underneath.

Darting away from him when he was about to put action behind the thought, she placed herself protectively behind a chair. "You'll have the rest of night when we come home for the birthday boy to get his gift."

"I'll be right back then." Laughing, Sal went upstairs to freshen up. Taking off his suit jacket and tie, he unbuttoned the first few buttons of his shirt, before running a comb through his hair before he went back downstairs where Valerie was waiting impatiently by the door.

"Finally!"

Sal shook his head at her. "I only took five minutes."

"Let's go," Grabbing him by the hand, Sal found himself having to speed up to keep up with her.

Eyeing her suspiciously in the elevator on the way down, he belatedly got the feeling that Valerie was up to something.

"You're not throwing me a birthday party, are you?"

Valerie shook her head. "No way. It's just going to be us tonight."

Satisfied with her answer, he allowed her to tug him out of the elevator.

Sal caught the happy smiles everyone gave him as they walked through the casino. When they came to the front door, they walked outside. Seeing them, one of the valets immediately walked over to them.

"Sal, I'll get your car for you."

"It's all right, Marco, I can get my own car. It's not that far of a walk."

"No need. It's slow right now. Vincent gets mad if he sees us standing around just talking."

After the incident with Valerie, Sal understood. The

last valet driver hadn't noticed that she was being held at gun point while she had been walked across the street to the Horseshoe. Not wanting to let another of Nadia's protégés get in trouble, he gave Marco his keys.

"Thanks, Sal. I'll be right back." The kid took off at a run.

Sal watched him go with a frown. He was going to have to have a talk with Lucca about Vincent.

All thoughts of Vincent were washed away as a car was pulled in front of Valerie and him. He had to blink twice at the car to make sure he wasn't imagining it. It looked like his car, but he instinctively knew it also wasn't. The car in front of him brought him eerily back to his tenth birthday.

When Marco jumped out, grinning, and tossed him the keys, Sal clumsily caught them, still awestruck.

"You've got a cool ride, Sal." Marco stood next to him, admiring the classic car.

"What do you think?" Valerie's quiet words had him turning to her.

"This isn't my car." It was, but it wasn't anymore.

"Yes, it is. Happy birthday, Sal!"

His mind still couldn't wrap around the fact of what he was staring at. There were so few happy memories he had of his mom, and the car had been a big part of them.

Walking forward to touch the hood of the car, he confirmed it was real and not a figment of his imagination.

"It's my mom's old car," he said, still in disbelief. There was no denying it, not even his replica brought him this much joy.

Valerie couldn't help but grin from ear to ear. "I saw the picture with you and your mom in front of the car, so I tracked it down."

Sal turned from his car in astonishment. "I did, too. I

tracked it down to a salvage yard. The worker I spoke to told me it had been crushed."

"You call or go there?" she asked, already knowing the answer.

He swallowed. "I called."

"I went there and showed the picture to the owner. Most of the parts had been parted out, but the owner couldn't bring himself to crush it. The car had been sitting in his garage for years. He had been planning on restoring it for his grandson. He didn't want to sell it to me ..."

Sal raised a brow. "How did you manage to get him to sell it to you, then?"

"I asked Lucca to talk to him for me," she said with a wink.

Sal looked back at the Casino Hotel to see Lucca standing behind the glass doors, watching him.

"Lucca found all the parts of the car that was missing and bought them," Valerie continued. "Maria found a car restorer for me, Nero bought the custom wheels, and Leo found the hood ornament."

Coming up to him, she put her arm around his waist. "The car isn't just from me but from all of your family, Sal. Even Vincent bought the original car mats, and Amo found the hardest part—the engine."

He didn't know what to say and couldn't have anyway from having the massive lump in his throat. With his gaze moving from Lucca's, he finally noticed all his family was there, watching him. They all then came out, seeing he had spotted them.

"What do you think?" Maria asked, joining them with his brother, Dominic, and their daughter. "Does it look just like you remember?"

Sal nodded with mist in his blue-black gaze.

"When I had it repainted, I thought you might like a different color this time around," Dante spoke around an unlit cigar. "But Valerie was adamant it had to be the same."

Angel, who had his arm hooked around Adalyn's shoulders, gave him an envelope. "The rest of us got together to give you plenty gas for a year and hand car washes."

Taking the envelope, it was hard not to get choked up. They all knew he didn't need the gift cards; he wasn't hurting for money. They had chipped in to show him they cared and that he was a member of the Luciano family, too.

Sal looked around the large group surrounding him in their midst to see just how much family he had accumulated for a boy who had been born homeless. "Thanks, everyone."

"You ready to go eat, son?" Dante asked, patting his shoulder.

Sal stared at his father then down at the woman who would make every birthday here on as special as his mother had when he was a child. "Where are we going?"

"So, I googled the hotel you told me you and your mom stayed at for your birthday, but the hotel has been torn down. It's just a casino now, but they have a buffet starting in twenty minutes. I reserved a whole section. Is that all right? If not"—Valerie gave him a mischievous smile—"we could always break in this bad boy with Taco Bell."

"And let you get lettuce all over my car?" Sal slung an arm around her shoulders, knowing she was joking, but just in case she wasn't ... "Hell no."

FAREWELL BLUE PARK

I'm homesick, and I can't sleep,
without seeing your face.
It's like going home,
when there's no place to go.
So, I look up at the moon,
And pray you aren't alone.
Like I am here in a new place,
Unable to go back home.

SARAH BRIANNE

*Please, if you or someone you know ever needs help,
follow this link to get more information and help.*

YOU ARE NOT ALONE.

victimsofcrime.org